SOMETHING BLUE FOR SOPHIE DREW

KATEY LOVELL

BLOODHOUND
BOOKS

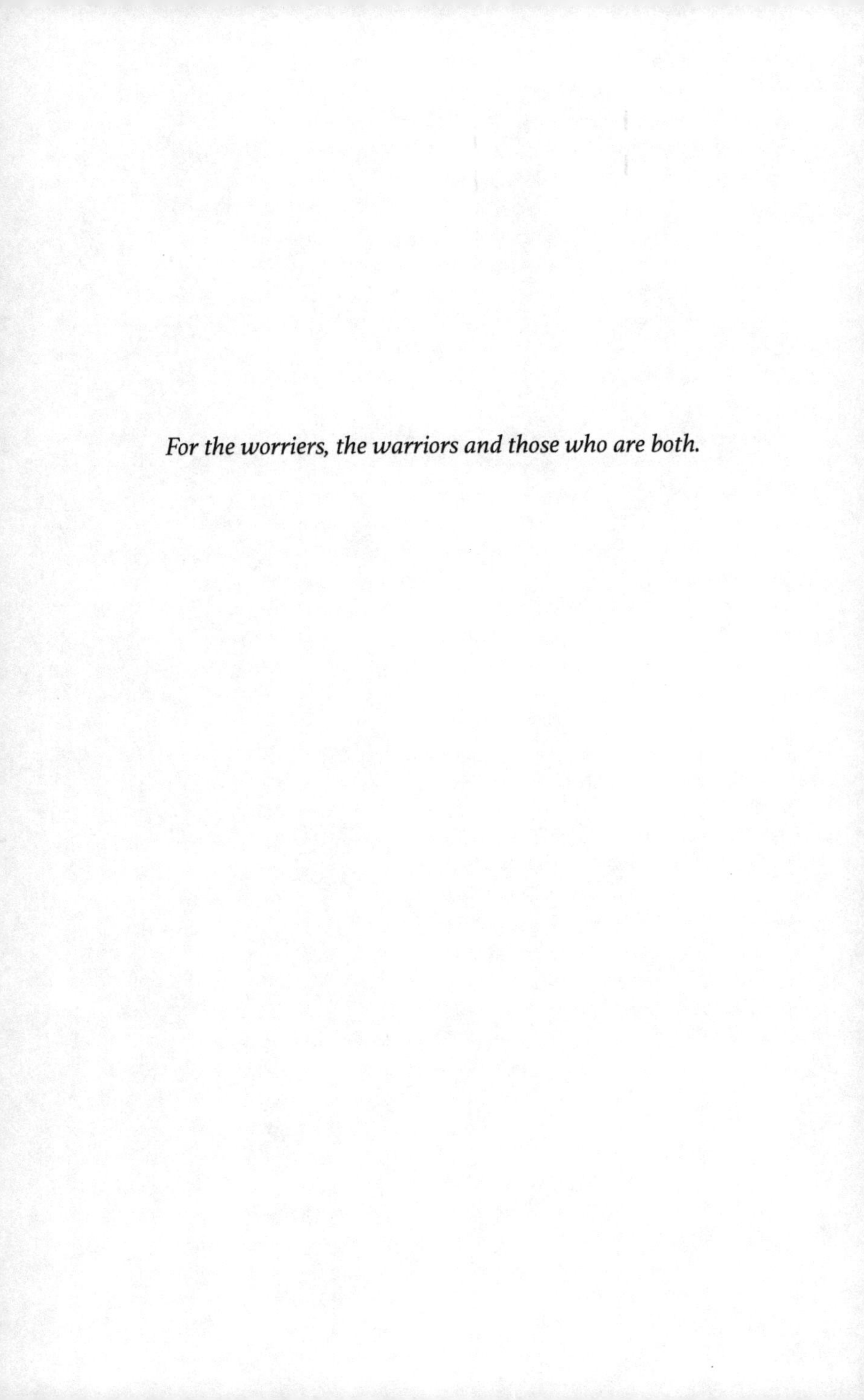

For the worriers, the warriors and those who are both.

thrown out of the window. We've been up since five and Scarlett was awake in the night three times."

Max yawned. Anyone else would have thought it was for effect, but as I was fighting exhaustion myself I knew it was for real. Naturally, I caught his yawn, what with the universal sign of exhaustion being more contagious than impetigo.

"But you're worth it, aren't you, Sugarplum?"

My fiancé reached out and gently smoothed his hand over our daughter's hair. Seeing the two of them together made my exhausted heart swell.

My family.

My own little family.

The rush of love was way beyond whatever I'd expected. My sister-in-law, Chantel, had told me it would floor me, but even so... Did every parent feel the same? Surely they must, but how did they ever manage to do anything other than care for their child? It was visceral, overpowering, this new type of love. I knew, without doubt, I would do anything within my power to keep Scarlett safe and care for her as best as I knew how to. Everything else would fall by the wayside.

My thoughts were still flying madly around my head (which seemed to be my new normal – ideas bouncing like the flat circular pucks on an air hockey table) when the familiar writhing began, the pink velour of Scarlett's Babygro shifting in Eve's arms. Scarlett's face crumpled, scrunching up until she looked like a little old man who'd removed his glasses and taken out his false teeth.

Her cheeks turned a shade or two darker than her name as she strained, angry determination in every push.

Next came the noise, a squelch squerch like in the book my parents had bought for Scarlett when they visited the hospital, followed by an unmistakable yet indescribable smell.

I knew what was going to happen next. The pattern was already predictable.

One...

Two...

Three...

"Waaaaaaaaaaah! Waaaaaaaaaaaah!"

My worn-out body went into overdrive, Scarlett's cries propelling me into action. I swooped forward, scooping her out of my friend's arms.

"Sorry," I said, with an apologetic grimace. "Nappy change time. She gets so upset when she's dirty."

"Hardly surprising, it can't be comfortable." A look of pity washed over Eve's face, her lips pressed together in a sympathetic line. "I wouldn't want to be sat in my own mess."

"Having a baby has made me think how hard it must be to rely on someone else for everything," Max mused. "No wonder babies cry all the time, it's their only means of communication. Must be so frustrating."

Eve responded with something sciency that I wouldn't have been able to process at the best of times and certainly not in my bleary-eyed state.

Max's inane nods at random points suggested he was also struggling to take her knowledge on board.

Escape was appealing.

"I'll just take her up. Back in a sec."

The waft climbed the stairs with us and I tried to place what it reminded me of. It was a strange smell; definitely excrement, but almost more animal than human. Cowpat, maybe? Or manure?

"Come on now." I laid Scarlett on the changing table, peeling back the poppers of her outfit before wrestling out her chunky legs. "No need to cry. You'll feel better once you've got a fresh nappy on."

As though on autopilot I ran through the sequence. Undo the nappy. Hold legs up with one hand, wet wipe in the other. Clean bum (always downward after the horror stories of infections). Pull out dirty nappy and slide a new one under my daughter's bottom end. Release legs, pulling the new stiff nappy into place. Seal the tabs. Fight legs back into the Babygro, do up the poppers. Fold the soiled nappy in on itself – my origami experience came in handy for that bit – and put it in a film-thin yellow sack that smelt of pound shop perfume. Tie the handles together. Dispose.

The first few times I'd been nervous. Although I had occasionally changed nappies before when I'd been looking after my brother's children, it was different with Scarlett. She was tiny. My hands seemed enormous by comparison and the fear of hurting her set me on edge, which was made worse by her habit of going rigid as soon as she pooed. Getting her out of her clothes was a challenge worthy of "The Crystal Maze".

When we were staying in the house I often dressed her in a long-sleeved vest and wrapped a blanket around her bottom half to keep her warm. It made changing her so much easier and I didn't have to panic that I might break a bone as I did when I forced her limbs out of the snuggly little sleepsuits.

It was different when people were visiting. They expected her to be fully clothed, preferably in whichever outfit they'd gifted. The house needed to be tidy. Everything was an effort.

Not to mention how much pressure I felt to make an effort myself. My skin was the worst it had been since my teenage years, the fluctuations in hormones causing painful acne breakouts on my face and neck. When half asleep my hands would automatically scratch the itchy patches and only when my fingertips were sticky with blood and pus would I realise what I'd been doing. I looked like I'd been mauled. Make-up would help, but my efforts applying it when drunk on sleep deprivation hadn't been successful.

There wasn't a word in the English language to encompass the overwhelming state of fatigue I was living in. "Drained" lacked the drama, "shattered" sounded too friendly. "Fucking exhausted" came close, but failed to capture how detached my brain felt from my body. "Zombiefied" was the only way to describe it. Half the time I wasn't one hundred per cent sure if I was awake or dreaming. A blast of cold water shocked me into action, I found, but it took more energy than I could muster to force myself into the shower in the morning. Even trudging to the sink to splash my face was a gargantuan task.

I'd taken to dressing in loungewear (new, two sizes larger than my pre-pregnancy clothes) when we were expecting guests. Comfy, but smart enough for in the house. In fact, during my pregnancy I'd noticed how the yummy mummies in the neighbourhood had adopted a similar look. Admittedly, their outfits were designer originals rather than Matalan knock-offs, but still... if comfort was good enough for them, it was good enough for me.

"Is that better?" I cooed, smiling to myself as Scarlett's lips puckered as though to blow a kiss. The cries had stopped once the nappy changing process was complete, my little girl as angelic as the two cherubs in that famous painting in the Sistine Chapel by Donatello. Or was it Raphael? Italian art wasn't my forte. One of the Teenage Mutant Ninja Turtles, anyway. "Better than that stinky nappy."

Taking the bag of waste in one hand and my daughter in the other I made my way back downstairs and dumped the plastic sack by the back door.

I paused as I reached the entrance to the lounge, taking a deep breath that caused my ribcage to lift high up towards my pocked chin.

"We've got this," I said to Scarlett who, once clean and content, was already close to sleep.

Then I plastered a smile on my face and opened the door.

CHAPTER 2

"Is this it forever?" Max yawned, stretching his arms above his head in an exaggerated fashion. "Starting the day at five isn't normal."

"You'd better get used to it," I insisted. "This is our new normal. For the foreseeable future we're going to be up at sunrise."

That was optimistic in itself. I'd been awake most of the night trying to feed.

Max placed his head in his hands, massaging his temple with his fingers. "I don't know if I can do this. It's hard enough now, how am I going to cope when I'm back at work?"

The whites of my fiancé's eyes were crazy-paved with red cracks, the result of being kept awake most of the night by our daughter's screaming. If the noise was loud by day it seemed worse still in the small hours of the night.

I empathised – my own head was pounding. What I wanted most of all was to pull the duvet over my head and catch up on the five hours of sleep I'd missed out on, but that wasn't an option. A teeny tiny human being was relying on me. There was only one thing for it, and that was dragging myself upright and forcing myself to get up and on with the day.

"I'm sorry, I shouldn't moan when you've been up all night too." Max smiled sympathetically. "Let me make you a coffee. And I won't hear any nonsense about it being something you should be cutting down on. The only way we're going to get through this is with the help of our old friend caffeine."

Max swung his legs out of bed and I could hear his heavy-legged stumble down the stairs as I tried once more to get Scarlett to feed. She grumbled, her lips feeling around my boob but without sufficiently connecting.

I knew pushing my nipple into her mouth wasn't the solution – there was more skill to breastfeeding than I'd ever thought possible. Angles were important, even in my exhausted state I remembered that much. Maths had never been my subject though. If I'd paid more attention in trigonometry class maybe I'd be better placed to (for want of a better phrase) get myself and Scarlett in a more successful position.

"One strong coffee, with plenty of sugar." Max placed a mug on the bedside table before glugging at his own hit of caffeine. "Yeowch." He pulled a face as he swallowed down his drink. "Too hot. Think I burned myself."

His upper lip was already turning from warm pink to poker-red. Max shuddered as he ran his finger over the sore area.

"Looks painful," I replied gently, as Scarlett clamped down on my breast. "I bet it'll blister, too. Maybe try putting Vaseline on it?"

"I'll get a drink of water to cool it down, but I bet it's going to blow up like a balloon."

As he trudged to the en suite I wondered, not for the first time, if we'd bitten off more than we could chew.

Scarlett chomped at my flesh, clueless. Even without teeth it was painful. Those gums were hard. Perhaps she'd bitten off more than she could chew too.

❧

I've always loved summer. Back in my wilder days it would hail the arrival of beer gardens and skimpy outfits, of rolling out of whichever club in town was the place of the moment as a new dawn broke across the sky. It meant shimmering lip gloss and coconut-scented sun cream, strappy sandals and trips to Europe's party islands. Ayia Napa, Ibiza, Magaluf... I'd done them all.

This summer was different, the long days signalling cups of tea on the patio rather than foam parties and drinking games. Not that I didn't appreciate it, because having a garden to spend time in was a godsend. Max had been right about our house – it was the ideal place for a family.

Max rocked from one foot to the other, his bare feet tapping against the patio tiles as he tried to make Scarlett burp. The rhythmic rapping of his hand against her Babygro-clad back was almost enough to lull me to sleep. Not that it would take much. The tiredness was like nothing else. I thought the party days would have been good preparation for sleepless nights, but apparently not. The coffee high didn't last long either.

"Go and have a lie down," Max insisted, not breaking stride with the beats. "We'll be fine out here, won't we, Scarlett?"

A perfectly timed and rather loud belch was our daughter's reply.

"Better out than in," Max quipped. "Right from the toes, that one. But I mean it, Soph, take a nap. You're dead on your feet."

"I don't think I'll be able to get to sleep, not with it being so light. You know I like it really dark."

Our bedroom curtains were thick material to start with, but

double-lined for good measure. I often wore an eye mask too, just in case any pesky light tried to ruin my slumber.

"You could sleep in the nursery?" Max suggested. "Those blackout blinds are supposed to be thick enough to block out anything, even this gorgeous sunshine. On the advert they wave a torch behind it and it doesn't show through. Go on, the nursery awaits!"

"I don't think I'll fit in the cot," I said, glugging the last of my tea (which was lukewarm at best) from my pint mug. The remnants of an earlier Rich Tea biscuit I'd dunked floated in the dregs. My stomach felt queasy at the sight.

"You know what I mean," Max replied with a laugh. "The nursing chair will be perfect for a nap. It's even got a footrest so you can put your feet up."

I didn't have the heart to say it wasn't my feet that were hurting. Whilst I'd expected the actual birth to be painful I hadn't bargained on the feeling lingering once our baby arrived. My foof was swollen – tender and raw – and even just sitting down felt like someone was stabbing needles into my nether regions. My friend, Mia, had loaned me a doughnut cushion – essentially an upholstered rubber ring – which took the edge off the agony when sitting, but only just.

When I'd mentioned the pain to the midwife she'd assured me that it was normal, a result of bruising caused by the birthing process, and suggested arnica would help. Max had very sweetly gone hunting for a chemist in search of nature's great anti-inflammatory.

What with the swelling and the endless bleeding I felt betrayed, like women everywhere had been lying by omission. Biology lessons hadn't prepared me for the onslaught of blood that followed birth. Lochia, the midwife called it. A bloody nightmare, I called it. You know what it felt like? Like the periods I'd missed through being pregnant had all descended at once. With tampons being out of the question (not that I'd want to put anything up there anyway) enormous pads were the order of the day. They reminded me of the sanitary towels my mum had bought me as a pre-teen "for when the time comes". They looked like big white bricks. I could have used them to make an igloo den, if I had the inclination. At least they offered some kind of padding, which I suppose was the purpose.

"You'll feel better for a sleep," Max assured me, still transferring his weight from one foot to the other as he rocked Scarlett. "Us two will be fine. There's an emergency bottle in the fridge, isn't there?"

I nodded wearily in response. We hadn't used bottles, so had no idea how Scarlett would respond to the alien object, but if she needed feeding it was there as an option.

"Exactly, and I've become a dab hand at nappies. Go on, have some sleep and then when you wake up I'll make us dinner. Risotto?"

Rest and food was an offer I couldn't refuse. "Okay." I moved gingerly. My body had gone through a trauma, after all.

If I'd had a car accident or an operation I'd be ordered to stay on bed rest as I recovered, but I'd quickly discovered giving birth was different. Women were out of hospital within hours of their bundle of joy arriving. It was one continual conveyor belt, popping out a baby then being chucked into the shark-infested deep end to get on with caring for them. My mum was horrified by how quick the process was these days. Her experiences had been very different, with a stay on the ward for a few nights being the norm. Only an emergency would be kept in so long nowadays. I remember one friend proudly telling me how she'd gone into hospital immediately after dropping her older child off at school, had the baby and was discharged in time to do the school pick up. Madness.

Each step to the house was uncomfortable, the chaffing

down below like carpet burns. I'd taken to slathering on the Sudocrem I'd bought in preparation, just in case Scarlett suffered with nappy rash, onto my nether regions. The cooling sensation offered momentary relief, which wasn't much but better than nothing. Never had I thought I'd be needing it rather than my newborn daughter.

My hand gripped the rail as I dragged myself up the stairs. My gait was all over the place, like that of a woman three times my age. I didn't trust my legs to keep me upright. Even my honorary Nanna Norma was spritelier, and she was in her eighties.

The soft talcum powder scent of non-biological washing powder hit me as I walked into the nursery.

Pushing the door closed behind me, I inhaled.

Peace.

Pulling the cord to lower the zebra print blackout blind, I exhaled.

Darkness.

Lowering myself into the chair, I inhaled once more.

Solitude.

Closing my eyes, I allowed my breathing to follow the same steady pattern and, before long, I was asleep, reclining on the nursing chair.

Two hours later, somewhat refreshed from my nap, I awoke to the sound of faraway chattering. At first I thought it was the radio, but quickly realised it was coming from the garden.

My mind raced as I ran through the "bookings" we had for visits. Everyone wanted to come and meet our new arrival, many of them armed with cards and gifts. It was lovely, but also relentless. Friends, family, workmates, neighbours... they were all desperate to meet Scarlett.

Me and Max had heard the phrases "we won't stay long" or "we'll pop in when we're passing to drop off a little something" so many times already. Everyone said they would only stay for five minutes to have a peep at the baby but I'd convinced myself it would seem rude if they didn't get to have a cup of tea and a hold (poor Scarlett being passed around like pass the parcel. Funnily enough, when she filled her nappy no one offered to unwrap her to see what prize awaited them, she'd be handed over sharpish with a comment about her crying for Mummy). It was as if our house had a revolving door, people coming and going all day long.

Cautiously, I made my way down the stairs and peered out of the kitchen and into the garden. If I hadn't seen it with my own eyes, I wouldn't have believed the scene in front of me. Not only were Max's parents there, so were two of his brothers, Dale and Chris, along with Chris's wife, Belinda. Andrea was revelling in her role as grandmother, cradling Scarlett with the self-assurance that can only come with having four children as Max poured what I assumed was the fresh apple and mango juice I'd been saving to have with a Netflix show during the middle-of-the-night feed (Good old *Gilmore Girls*, it can't be beaten) into the plastic beakers we'd bought for barbeque days.

The whole family gathering in our garden definitely hadn't been planned. I would have remembered.

Catching a glimpse of my reflection in the large mirror that hung in the back hallway, I grimaced. The power nap might have given me a recharge but it hadn't helped the bags under my eyes and my lank hair, scraped back into a ponytail because washing it seemed too big an effort. Not to mention the loungewear. Admittedly, it was clean on, but it was creased to high heaven from my nap. I couldn't face my soon-to-be-in-laws looking like I was ready to fall into bed. They would wonder what Max saw in me.

Every part of me wanted to go back to the safety of the nursery, shut the blind and hide away. When I was a teen I used to pretend to be asleep whenever my mum needed me to do any jobs around the house. It didn't always work as a get-out, but it did some of the time. The temptation to try the strategy again was immense.

Max's family are all lovely, but my home wasn't my own when they were around. How was I meant to relax? I'd been to parties with less guests. And although it was nice that the Oakleys wanted to see Scarlett, we never had this gush of visitors before she arrived.

She's our daughter, not some kind of fairground attraction that people roll up to see! I'd said similar to Max before and he'd laughed, not nastily, but enough to show he thought I was making a fuss.

My lips pursed together as I made my way back up the stairs. Any energy I'd gained from the nap was slipping away from me.

Resentment coursed through me as I groaned with the effort it took to remove my pyjama bottoms, and annoyance when I realised there was a smear of bright red blood on them where the brick-like pad had failed to do its job.

The salty sting of tears pricked at the back of my eyes as I stood statue still, the pyjamas pooled at my feet, blood-stained knickers staring back at me from the mirror that doubled as the wardrobe door.

This was supposed to be a joyous time, the happiest of my life. So why did everything feel so hard?

A long bohemian-style skirt (complete with a comfortable elasticated waist) and a loose-fitting top later, I was ready. Make-up hadn't been on the agenda, but I'd found a can of dry shampoo which freshened up my hair and I'd even added a squirt of perfume rather than just deodorant. It was the most effort I'd made since Scarlett's arrival.

"Look at you, Supermum." Belinda gave a tut of admiration. "You look great. It took me three weeks to get out of my pyjamas after giving birth to our Dylan. You put me to shame."

I mumbled back a comment about how it really wasn't that much of an effort, hoping my brave face went some way to disguising the smudges left behind by my tears. I'd heard about a celebrity who leant forward each time she cried so there was no trace of her tears and her fans and colleagues would be none the wiser. It was a technique I was already starting to master.

"You're doing so well, Sophie. You were cut out for motherhood." Andrea smiled encouragingly, still holding Scarlett. Where I was fearful of falling over when holding her, looking down at the ground with each cautious step I took, Andrea was a natural. It was as if she wasn't holding a baby at all. She was the one cut out for motherhood, not me. "It's not easy being a first-time mum, but this little sweetie looks happy and healthy, and a happy and healthy baby is all that matters."

I beamed back, biting my tongue when what I wanted to say was "what about me!"

Guilt crashed over me, strong and fast. What an awful thing to do, think about myself rather than my own daughter. Scarlett is so precious, so fragile. The love I have for her is almost unbearable, my heart is so full that every other relationship I've had pales into insignificance in comparison. My parents, Tawna and Eve, even Max... I love them all, but the fierce, protective instinct towards my daughter is like nothing else. She is my whole world in one furious little bundle, my raison d'être. The light of my life.

Yet still, I can't help feeling that when I gained a daughter I lost a part of myself.

"It's all change round here," Hector said. "New house, new baby, a wedding just around the corner. Exciting times for both of you. Or should I say for all three of you!"

"Oh, I don't think the wedding's going to be happening any time soon," Max said, taking Scarlett, who had just started to whimper, from his mother's arms. "Mum doesn't need to go hat shopping just yet."

"All the decent venues get booked up well in advance," Belinda advised, sagely. "Especially if you were planning on a summer wedding. That's what everyone wants, isn't it? Sunshine for the photos. If you've got somewhere special in mind it might be worth reserving a date. Two years in advance isn't out of the ordinary, you know."

Now, I like Belinda. She's friendly and has always made an effort to make me feel like part of the Oakley family. I assumed that was because she knew what it was like coming into such a tight-knit clan from the outside. But my word, she's a know-it-all. The subject matter makes no difference, Belinda's the authority on weddings, parenthood, whether flat shoes can ever be classed as "smart". Her opinion is the right one, and she has to have the final word.

Thankfully Max's mum interjected. "Give them a chance, they've only been engaged for five minutes."

Andrea threw a conspiratorial eye-roll in my direction. Maybe it wasn't just *my* nerves that Belinda was getting on after all.

"I haven't had time to think about what I'm having for tea, let alone planning a wedding. There's no rush. We've got the house, we've got Scarlett... a piece of paper isn't going to make any difference to our commitment to each other."

"Exactly," Max said firmly, smiling in my direction. "We're settling into life as a family of three first."

"Now you've got that ring on your finger everyone's going to keep asking you about the wedding whether you like it or not," Belinda said knowingly. She was persistent, and not in a good way. "It's like when you're pregnant and everyone wants to touch your bump. People see the rock and want to know how many bridesmaids you're having and whether it'll be melon or soup for the starter at the wedding breakfast."

"And we'll have answers to all those questions in good time," Max replied, his tone clearly drawing a line under the conversation.

It was hard work keeping the cheery smile on my face and a breezy tone in my voice, especially after Belinda acting like the ultimate authority on weddings, but I gave it my best shot. "Can you pour me a beaker of juice please, Chris? It's my favourite."

I maintained a sickly-sweet smile, even when the carton was drained before the cup was even half full.

CHAPTER 3

The shrill ring of the landline was a rude awakening, my eyes popping open wide as I fumbled for the handset, knocking a tube of nipple cream off the bedside cabinet in the process.

"Hello?"

"Soph, it's me! Are you all right? You sound a bit groggy."

There was no need to ask who it was. The spritely tinkle of Tawna's voice was so familiar.

"Yeah, well. I was napping. What time even is it?"

"Nearly six."

I looked at my watch, as though I didn't trust my friend's answer. Surely that wasn't right? I'd put my head down at four, hoping that resting my body would give me a boost.

"It can't be. I only meant to close my eyes for five minutes..."

"You must have needed the sleep. And why not? Make the most of being on maternity leave."

Tawna carried on jabbering but I switched off to the words, the bone-aching weariness throbbing through my body.

Being sociable had taken its toll. Once the Oakley clan had

left I'd climbed into bed fully clothed, letting Scarlett sleep next to me in the bedside cot.

Scarlett. It had been two hours since we'd gone to sleep and I hadn't heard a peep from her.

Panic coursed through me as I turned my head to my left. The cot was empty.

My mind went into overdrive yet I was frozen with fear. Had she managed to roll out somehow? The cot had bars around three sides, the only open side level with the bed where I'd been asleep. There was nowhere for her to go, surely. And although I was doing that thing parents do where they think their child is a genius, even I knew it would take a very advanced newborn to be able to roll themselves over however many times it would take to move a distance of at least a metre.

"MAX!" The shrill sound didn't seem to be coming from my body, but it was. "MAX!"

The phone fell from my hand, like a slo-mo scene in a TV drama, then clattered against the wooden floor.

Adrenalin surged through my veins, giving me the energy to scramble to my feet, the fear numbing me to the tiredness and the physical pain. All that mattered was Scarlett.

The most awful possibility raced through my mind in those dreadful seconds. She could have been snatched. Someone could hurt her. And it would all be my fault because I couldn't stay awake to keep her safe.

"MAX!" I repeated, shouting over the balustrade.

The soft pad of besocked feet danced across the wooden flooring in the hallway below.

As I leaned over the railing, a sigh of relief escaped my lips.

Max had Scarlett in his arms. She was fine. Safe.

But me? I wasn't doing so well.

CHAPTER 4

The shock stayed with me, even though I could see Scarlett was perfectly happy; the nervous prickling underneath my skin giving me the urge to scratch.

"She's fine," Max assured me. "She's been with me the whole time."

"I didn't know that, did I?" My jaw was set in a hard line, the surge of fight or flight adrenalin making me short-tempered. "I woke up and she was gone. I thought something awful had happened."

The furious panic refused to subside and Max, bless him, ordered I take a long soak in the bath.

"Take an hour for yourself to relax. Light some candles, use a whole bottle of bubble bath, I'll even bring you a glass of wine up if you like?"

I shook my head, vetoing the idea. It took every ounce of energy I could muster to run the bath, undress and clamber into the tub so the full home-spa experience sounded like a whole lot of effort. Plus, I was frightened I'd fall asleep the minute I sank into the water. I'd be no use to anyone if I drowned.

Once I was submerged, and got over the initial sting of the

water hitting my stitches, my mind began to wander. For the first time since Scarlett's arrival I allowed myself to think of something other than my daughter.

Andrea's comments about the wedding played on my mind – whilst I was of the mindset that there was no great rush, there was still the most important factor in the whole thing – that I actually wanted to be married to Max. I loved him, it was as simple as that. And Belinda had been so adamant that everything needed booking well in advance, so perhaps it was a good idea to begin making tentative arrangements.

Tawna's wedding had been a grand affair – a traditional church wedding with over a hundred guests followed by a reception at a country house hotel that had been attended by pretty much everyone she and Johnny had ever met. It had been a beautiful occasion, one that would live long in the memory of everyone who'd joined them for their special day.

I recalled how stroppy I'd been when Tawna had morphed from the kind-hearted girl I'd known since our schooldays into bridezilla extraordinaire. All she'd spoken about during the months leading up to the wedding were sugared almonds and table plans, bouquets and tiaras. It had been relentless, and whenever I'd spoken to her about it she'd quickly bristled, like an on-guard hedgehog, defensively stating how it was natural that, as a bride-to-be, she would want a perfect wedding. At the time I'd thought her ridiculous, overdramatic even.

With my own wedding on the cards I could see how planning could be a blessing. For Tawna, who doesn't work, it was something to focus on. For me, it might rekindle my stifled creativity. The wedding would be something I could put my energy into, that wouldn't be all about my newfound motherhood. Scarlett was brilliant. Bloody exhausting, but brilliant. But I wasn't ready to entirely give up my old self, to be a mother and nothing else. Perhaps planning a wedding would be exactly what I needed.

❧

"Are you sure about this?" Max's eyebrows furrowed until they disappeared behind the upper rim of his glasses. "It sounds like a lot of work and we're already adjusting to having Scarlett. Wouldn't it be better to wait a while, until we settle into being parents?"

I pushed my lips into a tight line and gave my fiancé the side-eye. "Anyone would think you'd changed your mind and didn't want to marry me after all."

Max sank down onto the settee next to me, lazily draping an arm around my shoulder as Scarlett fed, although "fussed" would be a more accurate description. Latching on was taking time for the pair of us to get the hang of.

"You know that's not true." The gentle lilt in his voice was full of affection. "I'd marry you tomorrow. I'd marry you now! I just remember how much time and effort it takes to arrange a wedding. Chris and Grant have both been through it and it was a mammoth task. An autumn wedding sounds great but October's not far away. Maybe next October would be more realistic. Places get booked up, don't they? That's what Belinda said. I want you to have the wedding you want, not compromise and then regret rushing."

I shook my head, the motion disrupting Scarlett. A low whimper started, almost like the bleating of a lamb, as her puckered lips struggled to find their way back towards my massive red nipple.

"Why wait? We know we want to marry each other so let's go for it. I know the perfect place for the ceremony, a secluded woodland, just for close family and friends. Then we can have a big party afterwards for everyone we want to join us."

"Sounds like you know exactly what you want."

"I do."

"Aren't you meant to save that to say that on the wedding day?" Max joked, as he fiddled with the fluffy material my dressing gown was made of.

His mischievous grin and the waggle of his eyebrows that followed made me laugh more than his terrible joke, he really did have the look of a naughty boy who'd been caught with his hand in the cookie jar.

Not for the first time I thought how lucky I was that I loved Max and he loved me back. Without him by my side I wouldn't be able to cope. Hats off to all the single parents out there, because it was hard enough with two people. Going it alone didn't bear thinking about.

I tried to hide my grimace as Scarlett clamped at my nipple, my toes curling with the pain.

One, two, three...

The first ten seconds were the hardest, I'd found. If I could just get through that, I'd be fine.

Four, five, six...

Tears swelled up behind my eyelids as the sudden sharpness took hold, like a million tiny needles jabbing at my breast.

Seven, eight, nine...

And just as I thought the pain was so excruciatingly awful that I couldn't bear it for one moment longer...

Ten.

It wasn't comfortable – the sensation not the natural, easy one I'd been expecting in my dreams of being a perfect earth mother – but it was no longer an unbearable agony and, most importantly, Scarlett was getting fed.

"An October wedding. This October," I reasserted, once me and Scarlett had established feeding. "I'll look into it tomorrow."

As I ran my hand over my daughter's head, marvelling how the hard bowling-ball skull had ever made its way out of my body, I focused on happy thoughts to encourage my breath to fall back into a comfortable rhythm.

Me and Max were getting married. Come October I'd be Sophie Oakley-Drew, and I couldn't wait.

JULY

Max's paternity leave was over far too quickly, and it took some getting used to being alone with Scarlett. There was so much to learn, and all to do when juggling a baby. Things that had seemed so easy when we were doing the practice runs, like putting the pram down, were much harder with Scarlett in tow.

Not being able to drive was another limiting factor. When we'd been able to hop in the car the world had been our oyster. In the time Max had been off day trips had included Durham, Saltburn and introducing Scarlett to The Angel of the North. We'd even taken her to St James's Park to buy her first football memorabilia, the cutest little teddy bear wearing a tiny version of the traditional black and white striped shirt of Newcastle United.

For the best part of a week I'd been planning a gentle walk around the green with the pram, telling myself it was the easy option. I'd put it off and put it off, but after three days of not leaving the house it was time to be brave.

First I changed Scarlett, putting her in a pretty cotton dress with matching sunhat. She looked adorable, even if I did say so myself. Max had left the pram ready in the hallway, with the sunshield ready to attach and I was quietly proud of myself for managing to fix it on first time.

My shoulders ached with exhaustion as I carefully placed Scarlett in the pram. Thankfully she was dozing and didn't scream the house down, which gave me time to apply sun cream to my face and neck and pull my hair into a ponytail.

It felt strange to be thinking about leaving the house. Home felt safe. It didn't matter that I was only planning a trip to the green, which I could see directly from the living room window. A nervous dryness filled my mouth as I opened the front door, the fresh air hitting me like a slap.

It was too much for me to contemplate. The neighbours would see me, judging my capability as a mother. I wasn't ready for the scrutiny.

Leaving the house wasn't an option, I'd only be proving how wet behind the ears I still was.

I closed the door. Indoors we were safe.

"All right, pet? How's your day been?"

I smiled to myself, the phone calls from my parents a highlight of my day. Adult conversation was limited, and although the conversations inevitably revolved around how well Scarlett was sleeping and feeding, it was comforting to know they cared.

"Same old same old." There was little else to report seeing as I wasn't leaving the house. Mum and Dad weren't really interested in how many reruns of *First Dates* I'd been watching during the long night feeds or how I was still scared of doing a number two in case the straining damaged my stitches even though the midwife had assured me they were healing nicely, but it was all I had to offer.

"Have you been out today? It's been boiling. We went to the pub for lunch and my nose is as red as Rudolph's now." Dad laughed heartily. "Serves me right for forgetting the sun cream. Hope you remembered yours."

"Don't worry, I remembered. Made sure I topped up before going out." Even though the furthest I'd gone was the back garden...

We made the usual small talk and I hoped I sounded bright and breezy, rather than imprisoned in the house, which was how I felt. Pretending everything was fine when it felt like I was hanging on by a thread was tiring.

That's why it was a nice surprise when Tawna called, I knew how to deflect her questions.

"Hello there, Mummy," she said, her voice light. "How're you all getting on?"

I repeated the same as I'd said to my dad half an hour earlier but was eager to hear about the outside world. No offence to my mum and dad, but Tawna's news was likely to be juicier than theirs (the big news in my parents' household being that the shower had started leaking so they'd called on Burly Bez, a friend of the family who happened to be a plumber, to sort it out. Hardly riveting stuff). "What's new with you?"

"Oh, you know. Just the usual, really." I could imagine her flicking her hand dismissively, mascara-coated eyelashes fluttering. "Hairdressers on Saturday. Tea with my mum yesterday at The Silk Room. Had far too much to drink, but sometimes it has to be done. Their cocktails are unbelievable, I had three Pina Coladas and pretended I was on holiday rather than in dreary old Newcastle." There was a momentary pause as she wracked her brain for any more news. "We're off to an awards do tomorrow night at the racecourse, Johnny's nominated in one of the categories. Can't remember which."

"What are you going to wear?"

Tawna's lifestyle meant she had hundreds of glamorous frocks, but I was sure she'd have bought something new for the occasion.

"It's a minidress, black sequins. Fancied something glitzy this time and as it's black tie me and Johnny will look good in the photos, it's always nice to match. The photographer from the paper will be there so I don't want to show Johnny up."

I poked at the soft doughy flesh of my belly as I thought of Tawna's slender figure and how she always managed to look like a film star. "Sssh. You know you always look amazing. And how's Eve? I've not heard from her this week."

"Snowed under. Did she tell you she's writing an article for a science journal? The deadline's next week so she's been glued to her laptop. Although she could do with a break and I did suggest popping round to see you and she was keen."

I couldn't hold back my smile, it would be great to see my friends. There was only so much one-way conversation I could have with Scarlett and although I adored Max, sometimes all you need is time with the girls. "I'd love to see you both, you're welcome any time."

"Perfect, I'll call Eve and see if she can come straight from work."

Knowing my friends were coming round made all the difference. It reminded me there was a life outside of the four walls of my house, a wonderful world full of opportunity and possibility that, with time, I hoped I'd be confident enough to navigate again.

Since Scarlett had arrived it had been impossible to switch off.

The day I'd woken up without her in the side cot had

exacerbated my overthinking. My mind had gone into hyperdrive with every little worry becoming a possible disaster. Hot drinks had the potential to scald, so tea and coffee were replaced by orange squash. Sleep was a no-no, even if I was barely able to keep my eyes open, because I was afraid of what might happen. Her being safe with Max last time didn't mean a thing, if the house was burgled someone could kidnap her. I even took her to the bathroom with me when I went to the toilet, scared to leave her in the Moses basket in case she fell out or stopped breathing or some other tragedy occurred. Being in sole charge of Scarlett was as terrifying a proposition as bungee jumping off the Tyne Bridge.

Seeing my friends would do me good, I was sure of that.

"You're doing brilliantly for a new mum," Eve assured me, as she gazed goofily at Scarlett. "It's really early days. You wouldn't go into a new workplace and expect to know everything, and it's the same with this, you're learning on the job. Stop being so hard on yourself."

"And look how content she is." Tawna was tracing her index finger down my daughter's cheek. "She's one happy baby."

Scarlett gurgled as though on cue, making both her honorary aunties "aww" at the cuteness.

Auntie Tawna had swooped in for a cuddle as soon as the pair had arrived, insisting she was entitled to first dibs on snuggles because she'd been there at Scarlett's birth.

They were both so thrilled to see her and so happy for me and Max that I felt bad for admitting it wasn't all smiles. I'd tried to tell my mum the same thing, especially after knowing she'd struggled to adjust to the demands of motherhood, but I couldn't find the right words.

I tried again.

"I'm worried in case something happens to Scarlett when Max is at work. Think how awful it'd be if she was maimed or worse..."

Eve laughed, but not with malice. "She's not going to be maimed. It's not like there are tigers and wildebeests roaming the streets of Newcastle looking for newborns to snack on."

"But you hear of these things. Not often, but they do happen."

"They do," Eve conceded, "but very, very rarely. I don't think you need to worry about it."

Her words did nothing to quell my anxiety. It was a maternal instinct, inbuilt and beyond my control.

"You're so precious, aren't you?" Tawna whispered, her eyes firmly fixed on my daughter. "So, so precious."

My heart panged for my friend; it must have been hard for her to hold a baby in her arms after her own recent experience. A painful reminder of what she'd lost. But there was nothing but love in her eyes as she cradled Scarlett, rocking her back and forth with an instinct so natural that I wondered if the universe had got it wrong, if she should have been the one with a baby rather than me.

"I don't want to be a nervous wreck, but it's hard not to see danger everywhere when you're responsible for a baby."

"You'll probably always worry. It's what mums do," Eve said.

'Gee, thanks.' I rolled my eyes, trying to imagine a lifetime of seeing the world through this new-found danger-vision. It was terrifying. "So I'm going to be like this for the rest of my life?"

The thought of continual worry along with lack of sleep for the next however many years was sobering.

"It'll get easier, once you two know each other better," Eve soothed. "She might not be able to talk yet but you still need to figure out what makes her tick and she needs to learn that you will always be there for her. There's all sorts of research about the mother/child bond and attachment theory."

She carried on talking her scientific bumph, her voice lulling me into a state where I was present in body only. My eyes were open, barely, but it was impossible to fully focus. I was awake but on the cusp of dreaming, asleep but aware of my two closest friends and my daughter's presence.

A veil of fog fell in front of my eyes, my vision hazed and Eve's chatter became more and more distant.

I was vaguely aware of Eve lifting my legs so they rested on the sofa, my body leaden, but it was as though I was watching the scene play out rather than living it first-hand.

Life carried on around me, Tawna resting Scarlett on the play mat on the floor as Eve made them both a cup of coffee. There was no energy in me to talk, not even to warn them about the dangers of hot drinks around my not-yet-mobile baby. Every ounce of life had been zapped out of me, but as the last hint of awareness vanished, a voice in my head kept saying the same thing over and over.

You're a terrible mother. You're a terrible mother. You're a terrible mother.

CHAPTER 6

"There she is, look," Eve cooed. She was cradling Scarlett, her hand supporting the weight of my daughter's head. "Mummy's awake now."

I jolted upright, blinking at the brightness as my eyes opened.

"What happened? Did I fall asleep?" My panic was evident in my voice, shrill and sharp.

"You shut your eyes for half an hour," Tawna confirmed. "You must have needed a power nap."

"No." I shook my head, my jaw slack. "I can't sleep in the day. Something could happen to Scarlett."

Eve let out a gentle sigh. "Nothing was going to happen to Scarlett. Me and Tawna were right here the whole time."

Two near-empty mugs were set down on the coffee table, no longer the danger they were when the liquid they contained was boiling hot, but a new fear flashed into my brain. What if a mug fell? It could smash, leaving sharp fractals of porcelain on the floor where Scarlett had her all-important tummy time, which the midwife said helped build the strength in her neck muscles. Hoovers aren't failsafe, even if I vacuumed thoroughly a shard

34

could be buried in the weave of the carpet. I would never be able to forgive myself if Scarlett cut herself because of my own inability to stay awake.

Why had I been so stupid and allowed myself to fall asleep?

"Hand her to me." My voice was abrupt and my arms stretched out for my baby. "She'll be starving."

"She's fine. She's been a really good girl, hardly made a peep the whole time you were asleep." Tawna's words were meant to be a comfort, I knew, but they weren't. If anything, I felt more clueless than ever.

Tawna and Eve left soon after, Eve making sure I'd taken a bite of the toast she'd prepared for me before she'd made her way out of the door. She'd slathered Max's favourite crunchy peanut butter onto the golden toast in a bid to up my protein intake.

"You need to look after yourself," she'd chided, watching as I sipped from the beaker of water she'd brought me. "How can you look after Scarlett if you're dehydrated and not eating enough?"

When Max had been at home he'd made sure I ate a sandwich every lunchtime so I was having something more substantial than chocolate digestives, but since he'd returned to work I'd fallen into bad habits, Scarlett's unpredictable routine meaning I often missed out on breakfast, lunch or both.

My nose crinkled as my sense of smell detected a telltale whiff. Nappy time.

Placing Scarlett on the plasticky changing mat, I stretched for the wicker basket of supplies. It was stuffed full with nappies, wipes and nappy sacks. I'd been so keen to use reusable nappies but the thought of having extra washing on top of everything else was too much. Maybe when she was a bit bigger, I thought, hopefully.

"That's better, isn't it?" I said in a babyish voice. "A nice clean bum ready for when Daddy gets home."

I snapped closed the poppers on her vest before wriggling her legs into the floral Babygro my sister-in-law, Chantel, had bought. It had been a peace offering after a strained few months where she'd been distant as she'd struggled to get over her difficult twin pregnancy.

The sound of Max's key in the door was a relief. The burden was shared. Not that Scarlett herself was a burden, but the weight of responsibility that came with looking after her... that was a burden of mammoth proportions.

"Honey, I'm home!" Max quipped.

The thud of his backpack landing on the wooden floor of the hallway was followed by the rustle of his jacket and as he walked into the lounge, his face shone with pride. From behind his glasses his eyes sparkled with love.

"How are my girls?" he asked, planting a fleeting kiss first on my forehead and then on Scarlett's before scooping her up into a bear hug. "Have you had a good day?"

I nodded, tight-lipped.

It *had* been a good day.

But, and it was a big but, I was exhausted.

"Tawna and Eve came around." I deliberately failed to mention the forty winks I'd taken. I didn't want Max to doubt my capabilities as a parent and worry about how me and Scarlett coped when he was at work. "It was nice to catch up."

"I bet Tawna was in her element talking about the wedding. She does love a big event."

A bolt of surprise shot through me. I hadn't even thought of the wedding, let alone spoken about it to the girls. My plans to ring around possible venues had fallen by the wayside too, the day lost to the endless cycle of feeding, winding and nappies.

"You've got the measure of her," I laughed, "but we didn't really talk about it." I shrugged. "Mostly they were just keen to see Scarlett. Tawna couldn't get over how much she'd grown."

"You're amazing, aren't you?" Max cooed, running the tip of his index finger down our daughter's cheek. "Everyone loves you."

Scarlett's lips parted with a quiet pop, curling up slightly at the corners.

"Look, she's smiling!" Max's own face was beaming, a look of pure adoration. "Definitely a proper smile too. You're a clever girl."

Scarlett let out a gurgle of joy in response.

A heaviness sat on my chest. It really did look like a smile, and the gurgle was almost a laugh. Scarlett seemed so happy with Max, so at ease, and it brought all my doubts back to the forefront of my mind.

I didn't let that show, instead laughing and saying, "She's a proper little daddy's girl, waiting until you get home to start showing off."

As Max sang a familiar nursery rhyme I found myself wondering how he made it all look so simple. He'd waltzed in, charmed our daughter and, in the process, left me feeling rather inadequate.

Bitter too, because Max seemed to enjoy all the lovely parts of parenthood while I was left to clean up explosive poos, drag my exhausted body out of bed for night feeds and deal with the nagging worries that, no matter how hard I tried, I was never going to be the perfect mum Scarlett deserved.

CHAPTER 7

The following day was everything you'd hope for summer – endless blue skies, the sun's warmth prickling against bare skin, the scent of roses and lavender drifting on the gentle breeze.

I'd made sure to arrange for visitors to call by each day, thinking it would be the kick up the bum I needed to get washed and dressed (even though the comfort of my pyjamas spoke to my heart).

Iris, Jude and baby Dana arrived just before lunch, which also coincided with Scarlett waking up from her morning nap.

Jude toddled around the garden, chasing the cabbage white butterflies that had appeared en masse when the weather turned warm. Compared to Dana and Scarlett he looked enormous, and when I tried to picture the girls at that age it was impossible. Iris was settled in the hanging egg chair, feeding Dana with an expertise I envied. Scarlett's continual fussing, not to mention the cracked nipples and latching-on pains, still had me dreading every feed.

"So," Iris said, looking every inch the serene earth mother in her loose cotton trousers and floaty top, "how are you doing?" I opened my mouth to speak but before I could say a word she added, "And I don't want any of the bullshit you tell other people about how it's great and you're loving every minute. Being a parent is rough, especially if you're the one who's given birth. Your body's been through a lot over nine months, and then the birth..."

"I'm fine." My voice was breezy and I even threw in a smile for good measure.

The look Iris gave me in return could only be described as "knowing", but she didn't press further. I suspect she knew I was close to breaking point and that, in my fragile state, it wouldn't take much for me to crumble.

"I'll tell you something, I'm bloody knackered." Her Aussie accent sounded stronger than ever. "Dana's teething, I'm sure of it. There's no sign of any teeth yet but her gums are rock solid and she's screaming blue murder during the night. We've tried all the powders and a teething ring that's been in the fridge but nothing's working. I hate to think of her being in so much pain."

"Poor thing, I remember how it felt when my wisdom teeth were coming through. If it's anything like that then it's no surprise she's crying."

"I feel sorry for her but the minute she starts we're all wide awake. Then her crying sets Jude off so me and Jessie end up with one child each. Then we end up bickering about who's got off the easiest because at least Jude calms down once he's got his favourite toy elephant to cuddle. Dana on the other hand... she's strong-willed. I dread to think what she's going to be like when she's older. Stubborn as a mule."

My friend shuddered, and a part of me withered away. This was just the beginning. Teething, toileting, weaning... this was all to come, each bringing with it a unique set of challenges.

So many potential mistakes, so much for me to mess up.

I glanced over to Scarlett, awake, but lying peacefully in the

Moses basket. The fear that I was letting her down swelled up inside me again, bubbling away like molten lava.

Iris snapped her fingers, pulling me back from my thoughts.

"Earth to Sophie," she said with a shake of her head. "You were miles away. I know my moaning is boring but still! You could at least pretend to be interested!"

"Sorry. It's nothing personal. Probably the lack of sleep catching up with me."

I shrugged, hoping the apology was acceptable.

"I know that feeling." Iris gave a sympathetic smile. "Everything's harder when you're tired."

"And you and Jessie have two of them ganging up on you." I shook my head, trying to imagine how hard it must be. It was difficult enough with one. Having another child so soon after Jude must mean they were either perfect mums or more tolerant than I was ever likely to be. One was enough. One was more than enough. "I don't know how you do it."

This time it was Iris's turn to shrug. "There's no other option. We just have to get up and get on with it, remembering what everyone says, that they don't stay little for long. When they're teenagers we'll be nagging them to get up in a morning rather than praying they'll settle down at night."

"I used to lie in bed until lunchtime every weekend," I recalled, "especially when me, Eve and Tawna had sleepovers. We'd stay up talking until the early hours then sleep in as late as we could. I remember this one time Eve's mum woke us up and it was one o'clock. She had lunch on the table for us!"

I laughed fondly at the memory. Those times had been so happy, so carefree. We hadn't realised then how difficult adulthood was, with holding down jobs, running a home, finances and families... Ignorance had been bliss.

"What I wouldn't give to be able to have a proper night's sleep now..." I glanced in Scarlett's direction.

"Is Max getting up with her at all? I know it's hard when you're the one feeding, but if you express Max could give her a bottle?"

"If only," I scoffed, as Scarlett started to wriggle in the bassinet. "We haven't tried her with a bottle yet. Plus, Max sleeps so deeply he doesn't even notice she's crying half the time."

Iris's face contorted. "Are you sure he's not pulling your leg? When Dana's throwing a hissy fit the whole street knows about it and I bet Scarlett's the same. They're noisy little blighters."

"Honestly, he's so tired by the time he gets into bed that I don't think he's messing about. He's working really hard at the minute and then when he gets home he wants to spend time with Scarlett, which I get. I'd want to spend time with her if I was the one out at work all day. But by the time he's done her bath and had his tea he's shattered. It's all I can do to stop him crawling up to bed at eight. Half the time he falls asleep on the settee when we're watching telly."

Iris's brow furrowed. "And you're okay with that? I'd be raging mad if Jessie wasn't pulling her weight. The nightshift is a toughie, but just because he's working doesn't mean he has a get out of jail free card."

A little squawk came from the Moses basket. Scarlett was wriggling again, her puce face scrunched up like a wrinkly cabbage. The poonami was coming. Opening her bowels seemed to be a major cause of stress in my daughter's life and, as usual, the squawk soon became a full on wail.

"It's all right, sweetheart," I soothed, picking her up and cradling her close to my chest. "Mummy's here."

"Look at her grumpy face." Iris wasn't being mean, there was affection in her tone. "She looks so sad."

"It's the pooing," I explained as Scarlett strained once more, her face now the colour of a Victoria plum. "She hates it."

I'd hoped Iris might have some words of wisdom to share,

but even if she had they'd have been drowned out by Scarlett's cry. The noise was accompanied by a smell that suggested Scarlett had achieved what she'd set out to, and even Jude, who'd been happily entertaining himself as me and Iris had been chatting away, wafted his hand in front of his nose and said, "Pooey."

Apologetically, I took my stinky-bummed daughter into the house to change her nappy, pressure building up behind my eyes. It was relentless, a Groundhog Day of nappies and feeds. I was hanging on by a thread, but I couldn't tell anyone how anxious I was feeling. At what stage did social services get involved? Would someone take Scarlett away if they knew how much I was struggling?

My vision blurred as I lay Scarlett, stripped down to her vest, on the changing mat, fat teardrops falling from my eyes and landing on my daughter's chubby thighs.

"I'm sorry." The words came out strangled. "I'm sorry. You deserve a better mum than me."

It was hard to change her properly whilst overcome with tears and through it all I was, for the first time, grateful I was using disposable nappies. In my fragile state fiddling about with liners and wraps would have tipped me over the edge.

Scarlett's vivid colour had calmed, her cheeks a flushed rosy pink rather than the angry shade of purple they'd been at the height of her rage. She looked up at me with curiosity and innocence.

"That's better, darling, isn't it?" I said, mopping up the mess with a wet wipe before pulling another and dragging the cool damp cloth across my eyes. "Mummy's doing the best she can."

And I really was doing my best, so why did it feel that it wasn't enough?

CHAPTER 8

Sometimes, I realised, you can try with all your might and it will still never be enough. That's exactly how it felt each day when Scarlett's caterwauling started the minute Max walked out of the door. The cry was like nothing else, shrill and ear piercing. Whether it was a mother's instinct or some other guttural reaction I don't know, but the knots in my stomach made me want to vomit. I was living on my nerves.

In those moments I could see why parents sometimes did things that seemed crazy to the outside world. It was so, so tempting to walk out the door and leave Scarlett and her crying behind. I never acted on it, but I understood how in a moment of desperation parents might make choices they never normally would.

Was I a terrible person for feeling empathy towards parents who had left their child alone? And I wouldn't ever dream of hurting my daughter but I could understand how someone might reach the end of their rope and shake their baby to try to end the dreadful noise.

I laughed when a daytime talk show ran a feature about people using the controlled crying method. Were those people mad? They had to be. No one in their right mind could put up with it. I'd do anything within my power to stop Scarlett when she was on one. I'd sing to her, everything from traditional lullabies to "Wannabe" by the Spice Girls.

Place her stomach down over my arm as though she was flying a la Superman. This was a trick Rachel had recommended but it wasn't as successful for us as it seemed to be for the other mums I knew. Nothing seemed to stop Scarlett from crying once she was in her stride. Infacol helped slightly, although maybe it was a placebo effect and I just wanted to believe it helped. I didn't even know for sure if it was colic which was causing the pain or if it was something else making her distressed. All I knew was neither me nor my daughter could carry on like this.

"Have you thought about cranial osteopathy?" Iris had asked, always one to suggest alternatives. "We tried it with Jude and even though we weren't sure it would work, it did help. Me and Jessie had reached breaking point and then the osteopath laid his magic hands on Jude and we had a full night's sleep. We were like new women."

I was at the point where I'd try anything. I couldn't carry on snapping as often as I was over the silliest things. Patience had never been my strongest point but the lack of sleep and seemingly continual crying was almost unbearable. I went ballistic at Max when he returned from the supermarket with a different brand of toothpaste to my usual favourite and then had to contend with the guilt that accompanied my outburst.

Things that wouldn't normally affect me had a huge impact. The adverts on the TV, the ones for UNICEF and similar charities where children are shown with no clothes, water or shelter seemed as though they were targeted directly at me now I was a mum. The campaigners knew what they were doing, it was out and out manipulation. I'd sob my heart out as I cradled my beautiful screaming child to my chest, both of us inconsolable.

I cried down the phone to the receptionist at the osteopath's. She only sounded like a young girl, but she was calm and must have been able to pick up on my desperation because she managed to fit me and Scarlett in for an appointment the very next day.

"You're in luck, we've had a cancellation," she explained. "You rang at the right time."

I could have jumped for joy, I believed the osteopath might be the beginning of the end to the constant crying.

With Max out all day and the thought of taking a screaming Scarlett anywhere bringing me out in a cold sweat, I made the decision a duvet day was in order. Trailing the bedding downstairs behind me, I set up a camp for us on the settee surrounded by emergency snacks for me and I bought books and rattles for Scarlett.

Knowing I'd be out the following day, I allowed myself to spend the day in our own blanket fort without beating myself up (too much).

We curled up in a cocoon like caterpillars waiting to emerge as butterflies. It was cosy and safe and although Scarlett was still grumpy she must have picked up on the good vibes too because her wails were less of a piercing shriek and more akin to how other upset babies sounded. I wondered if the safety of the duvet reminded her of being wrapped up and warm in my womb, her body against my chest so we could feel each other's beating hearts.

I reached for the remote.

"You've got to be kidding me."

My words were a barely audible mutter and my tut was out and out disgust, but I didn't do the sensible thing and flick onto another channel. Oh no, instead I kept watching the daytime film on terrestrial TV even though I'd never liked it as a kid, let alone as an adult.

I began a tirade against the irritating girl in the film, even though there was no one except Scarlett to hear me whining.

"This is 'Annie'," I started, "and it's one of the most saccharine things you'll ever see."

Scarlett stared at me, and I took it as a sign to continue as "Hard Knock Life" played out in the background.

"Even at the beginning when her life's terrible she's happy-go-lucky like a chirpy little leprechaun, if you can get American leprechauns. It's unrealistic. I know that's the whole point of the film. Fighting against adversity and all that. But painting a smile on regardless of how you're actually feeling isn't the right thing to do."

I let out a sigh and pulled the duvet more tightly around me. Then I pointed the remote at the TV, forcefully pressing the channel button. That was enough of that. Instead I watched old favourites I could depend on, programmes that didn't rely on a millionaire sweeping in to save the day.

We stayed there all afternoon, watching the comforting TV shows I'd seen over and over. My favourite episode of *Gilmore Girls*, the one with the road trip to Harvard, and episodes of *Friends* that never got old and had the ability to raise a smile anytime I was at my lowest.

Max got home from work to find us still cosied up and although there wasn't much room with all our necessities taking up space he dived right under the covers with us before he'd even taken off his shoes. It was a squash, getting us all on our sofa, but a happy one.

"How was your day?"

I always made a point of asking, seeing as he was the one out at work.

"Oh, you know. The usual madness that comes with working

in a charity shop. Poor Gemma got the shock of her life first thing when she opened up a bag of donations to find a dildo shoved in there."

"Urgh." I pulled a face. "That's disgusting."

"She thought it was weird," Max continued, "but the freakiest part was it was in a carrier bag of cuddly toys. We were about to dispose of it when a woman came charging back through the doors demanding her bag. Turned out she had two of those big Aldi carrier bags and the one she meant to donate was full of CDs. I don't know who was most mortified, Gemma or the woman."

"At least she came back, I suppose. And donating CDs is less offensive than a dildo."

Max cocked one eyebrow. "I don't know about that, there were a few Daniel O'Donnell albums in her collection."

"Weird that the sex toy was in with a load of teddies," I said thoughtfully.

"That's not all. There were some giant nappies too."

Max gave me a knowing look.

"Oh." Realisation dawned. "Like those couples on the telly who pretend to be mummy and baby?"

Max shrugged. "Don't ask me, I'm not into role play. That's what Gemma thought too though. She wondered if it was some kind of pervy game."

"After working with Kath I'm pretty clued up on that kind of thing. If you've heard about it, she's tried it. Even if you haven't heard about it she's probably tried it. I don't know half of the stuff she does. A couple of months back she was talking about Monkey Face. I thought she'd made it up to make a point about how vanilla the rest of us in the office are, but turns out it's a thing."

Max looked at me, a questioning frown etched on his handsome face.

"You don't want to know," I insisted. "If I could go back in time and erase it from my memory, I would."

"Tease. You can't say something like that and expect me to let it go. If you won't tell me I'll have to Google it and if I die it'll be on my search history and everyone will think it's something we're into."

"Google it at your peril," I warned. "And don't blame me if it gives you nightmares."

He should have heeded my advice rather than pulling out his phone and typing the phrase into the search engine.

"That's gross. Do people really do this stuff?"

I shrugged. "Don't ask me, it might be an urban myth."

"Or it might be true..." His voice trailed off and I could sense his brain processing.

After what seemed like an age, when he'd finished pondering the likelihood of the bizarre sexual act being something practised up and down the country, I told him about the cranial osteopathy appointment.

"You probably think it's nonsense but I'm willing to give anything a try. Iris said Jude slept through after his sessions. Imagine if Scarlett did that!"

I knew it was a pipe dream, but still... the thought of an uninterrupted night's sleep sounded heavenly.

"Imagine," Max echoed, as he closed his eyes and tilted his head back against the settee. "Imagine."

CHAPTER 9

The cranial osteopathy clinic was based on the ground floor of a stone house that had been converted into offices. On the upper floor there was a counselling centre. I wondered if that was where they sent the parents of the children the osteopath couldn't "fix".

An impressively heavy door opened into a muted white corridor with steel grey dado rail and door frames. A bell jangled as we entered and climbed the step that led to the raised area where the receptionist perched behind a desk. Not the one I'd spoken to when booking the appointment, unless I'd misjudged her age. The lady had perfectly coiffured black hair and eyebrows that were very definitely drawn on rather than natural.

"Welcome to Stonemont." Her voice washed over me, blending in with the gentle classical music playing in the background. She smiled, her lips curling upwards. "Do you have an appointment?"

I explained I'd booked a last-minute cancellation and she pulled Scarlett's information up on the computer.

"If you'd like to take a seat in the waiting area you'll be called through when Simon's ready for you."

It all sounded very informal considering the amount it was costing. I'd expected him to be referred to as Doctor or Mr Taylor at the very least. Simon sounded so... ordinary.

Typically, Scarlett didn't make a peep. She'd been quiet and settled on the journey too, where she'd been strapped to my chest in the sling – I was glad the appointment had been early because it meant Max had been able to help me put the bloody thing on. It was a hellish contraption of clips and straps that looked like an instrument of torture rather than a baby carrier (at least, it would if it wasn't for the pastel floral print).

I allowed myself to close my eyes and relax as the music played softly. I knew the tune, it was one that had been used on an advert a few years ago.

"Scarlett Oakley-Drew?"

A man in a navy tunic and trouser set appeared. He had a kind face, round and ruddy, and I trusted him immediately. He looked dependable.

"Here." I raised my hand the way I had done back in my school days. "She's just dozing."

"Come through to the consulting room," he said, guiding the way, "and we'll see what we can do to help."

"I'm Simon, by the way," he said as he invited me to take a seat. His demeanour was calming, reassuring. "So tell me all about Scarlett."

I proceeded by waffling, glad to have a professional to offload on. I shared the sleepless nights and the heartbreaking crying and was about to unstrap my sleeping daughter when he stopped me.

"Don't wake her unless you were going to anyway, I can do what I need to do with her in the sling, so long as you don't mind me leaning across you."

It was a bit weird having someone I'd only just met manoeuvring my body so he could place his hands on Scarlett, and the whole process was far less clinical than I'd expected.

Without touching me at all, the warmth of his body reflected back from mine. A sensation I recognised rippled through me, starting in the pit of my stomach and then gravitating downwards until the tingle between my legs caused me to catch my breath. Could he tell the effect he was having on me? It was almost spiritual, and I was momentarily unaware of him holding his hand against Scarlett's head in what was more of a massage than a clinical procedure. Everything was heightened – Simon's body curved around mine, the tickle of his breath behind my ear, my own breathing becoming more and more shallow as the feeling intensified.

Then, just like that it was all over.

"Hopefully that'll do the trick, but sometimes it does take multiple sessions." The fire was still burning in my underwear. "If you need to book in again mention that you've been before. Registered clients get priority over newbies."

As I handed my bank card to the receptionist to pay for the session, I was doubtful that something so simple would make any difference whatsoever to Scarlett's woes. The whole experience had lasted ten minutes at most, Scarlett hadn't even had time to stir.

Me on the other hand... I was well and truly stirred.

I called Iris on the way to the bus stop, jokingly calling her a hippy for buying into the whole thing, when what I really wanted to ask was if she'd experienced the whole Stingtastic tantric sex thing too.

"If it works for you as well as it did for us you'll be thanking me for introducing you to Simon Taylor."

I hoped she was right.

CHAPTER 10

*B*y the following week I'd beaten myself up every day about not being good enough. All I could think about was that Scarlett was so reliant on me and the pressure, the unbearable pressure, of keeping her nurtured and safe scratched at my insides.

Guests were still visiting – Nick and Chantel were regulars, as were both mine and Max's parents – but I was still aware of the fact I'd promised to pop into work so everyone there could meet the new arrival.

Lunchtime would be the best time to go, when people had time to chat and have a hold, I decided, setting it as a goal. As six o'clock starts were the new normal that gave me plenty of time to savour a cup of coffee (only one, because I could throw it down my neck as Max watched over Scarlett. Anyway, any more than that disagreed with her delicate digestive system). I needed to ensure the changing bag was fully stocked before heading out to the office too, but a whole morning should be more than enough.

As it happened, there wasn't plenty of time. Norma arrived on the doorstep weighed down by a home-made loaf of banana bread and a bunch of mixed roses. It had slipped my mind that she was coming around, but I ushered her through to the lounge, put on both the kettle and a smile and acted as though I'd been waiting for her arrival.

"Look at how big she's getting." Norma stroked my daughter's shock of hair and Scarlett let out a gurgle of delight. "You're doing brilliantly, Sophie. She's a lucky girl having a mum like you."

The sting of tears prickled, failure yet again snapping at my heels. Since the osteopathy session Scarlett hadn't been quite so fraught, but trying to give my daughter my all while running on empty was taking its toll.

"Your mam was telling me you're organising the wedding too. Talk about not doing things by halves." She laughed. "Mind you," she added, lowering her voice to a conspiratorial whisper despite there being no one else within earshot, "our wedding was a quickie too. Didn't have much choice because I got caught out. In those days there wasn't the option of waiting."

I gawped. Norma was old, but not that old. Brian, her son, was in his mid to late fifties so, if my mental maths was right, that would mean Norma and Fred got married in the late 1960s, or early 1970s at a push.

"Don't look so shocked. I know you youngsters don't understand what it was like but you've got to remember that when people talk about the swinging sixties it wasn't all like that. My parents, God bless their souls, were born before the First World War. The generation above mine had very traditional values. It would have broken my dad's heart if I'd had a child out of wedlock."

I tried to imagine what that must have been like. Other than people assuming my surname was hyphenated the same as Scarlett's there had been no judgement at all about me and Max not being married, which was hardly surprising as so many of the people I went to school with had children without a ring on their finger.

"Anyhow," she continued, "tell me everything about this wedding of yours. What have you planned so far? Church or hotel for the ceremony? I know you're not religious but there is something special about a church wedding. And what about colour schemes? If you're dead set on autumn perhaps rich purples and oranges would be nice..."

The laugh escaped without me thinking about it – Norma seemed to think it was arranged down to the last detail when the truth was I'd still done nothing. It wasn't because of lack of enthusiasm, more a lack of energy. The exhaustion never seemed to dissipate, even when I climbed into bed the minute Max walked through the door. I'd tried everything to boost my energy levels, from vitamin pills to cans of Red Bull, but nothing was a match for my weariness.

"I've not had the time to get much done yet, but I've got a list up here of what needs doing." I tapped the side of my head with my index finger. "I've been watching those wedding shows on the telly though, hoping to steal some ideas."

They were the perfect distraction when breastfeeding. *Married at First Sight, Don't Tell the Bride, Say Yes to the Dress* – all the trashy reality TV I loved and I could class it as research. Some of the weddings were awful, not what I'd had in mind for me and Max, but there were elements of each that appealed to me. The notes app on my phone was full of random comments like "are sunflowers still in bloom in October?" and "spit roast?", all gleaned from my TV habit rather than the glossy magazines Tawna had been a slave to when she was planning her wedding.

"Oh, Sophie." Norma tutted. "Don't go watching that nonsense and filling your head with these fancy ideas. In my day weddings weren't about how much money you spent, not like they are today. It was about the love."

"It's still about the love," I said with a laugh. "That's why people get married in the first place."

"But it's the showy wedding that they're focused on. People take years planning one day." She shook her head, her thinning brilliant-white hair not moving a millimetre after her weekly style and set. "It's the marriage they should be thinking of, not the wedding."

"You can't blame people wanting a day to remember. It's not as though people get married every day. For most it's a one-off experience."

"Me and Fred didn't have an all singing and all dancing affair, but it was still a perfect day. I can remember it down to every last detail. And we didn't have hundreds of photos like the youngsters do now. When Brian got married we paid for a photographer. Two thousand pounds and that was twelve years ago!"

She shook her head once more, her lips in a tight, disapproving line. "No thank you, not for me. Family took black-and-white snaps for me and Fred and that's enough. The important memories are up here." It was her turn to drum her index finger against her temple. "Don't fall into the trap of thinking everything needs to be just so, Sophie. I've seen how you and Max look at each other, like you're each other's world. That's what's important, not all the other stuff. You remember that."

"I will," I promised, "don't you worry."

&
&

It was funny, talking with Norma started me thinking about weddings, and once I started I found it near impossible to stop. I made a point of ringing around the venues that interested me, fooling myself into believing it was only a first enquiry to find out prices and availability. The truth was, after devoting hour upon hour to watching every wedding programme going I was beginning to catch the bug. However, I was determined not to fall into the trap so many brides before me had succumbed to by letting dreams of their big day run away with them. Our wedding would be a reflection of us as a couple and we had worked hard to pay off previous debts. Neither of us could see any reason to spend a crazy amount of money.

Max had been horrified when I'd dropped the average cost of a UK wedding into conversation. The colour drained from his cheeks and I suspected he regretted telling me that he'd be happy with whatever I wanted.

"Twenty-seven thousand pounds? Are you sure? That's more than I earn in a year."

"Yep, I know, it's madness. Easy to see how people get caught up in it though. The calls I've made show how quickly it can snowball."

My notebook was filling nicely with quotes, and any moment Scarlett was asleep was dedicated to the hunt for a venue.

Max was delighted with my progress and I was almost proud to have whittled down my conversations to a top-three list. My first choice was still a rustic wedding in the woodlands, followed by a quiet and tasteful tea party in a marquee for close friends and family. A big knees-up in the evening would round off our special day.

"I'm just happy that you're excited," Max said, after I'd filled him in on the information I'd garnered.

"Of course I'm excited," I scoffed. "There's nothing I want more than to be your wife but I hadn't bargained for the amount of work it takes to plan a wedding. This was just venues and it took most of the day."

I'd always mocked people who'd hired wedding planners,

but from dipping my toes into the water of arranging such a large event I was beginning to see their appeal. Finding a place to get married was the first step of the process and I already had a mess of notes on prices and options. I could see how getting multiple quotes for each and every facet would be time-consuming, not to mention confusing.

"We should probably arrange to visit your favourites," Max said thoughtfully, but I was one step ahead of him.

"I've made appointments for us to go and see three on Sunday. Parring Hall first, then Cotterly Manor, and the woodland in the afternoon."

Max nodded, and I could tell from his expression he was impressed. "You really have been busy. Scarlett must have been a good girl today to let Mummy get on with phoning around."

"She's been as good as gold." And she had been, happily watching her mobile and listening to the jingly version of "Somewhere over the Rainbow" that it played on repeat. Other than changing her nappy and feeding she'd been very low maintenance all day. "I was showing her the photos of the woodland on their website. Did you know it's home to pipistrelle bats?" I hadn't known what they were until I'd seen them on the internet, but they were so cute. "And foxes, and badgers."

Although it made sense not to jump ahead until we'd seen the venues in person, I already had my heart set on the woodland glade. I just wasn't a country house kind of girl and my lack of religious beliefs made me feel that to marry in a church would be hypocritical. The last time I'd gone to church for an event other than a funeral or a wedding was probably at high school when we had performed as a school choir at a fundraising event. Well, I say performed... I was told to mouth the words because no matter how hard I tried I was always off-key.

"I really like the idea of the woods," I said, my voice

sounding almost questioning. I didn't want Max to think I was taking control of the situation without giving him a chance to contribute. Weddings might often be seen as a woman's interest but our wedding was going to be a big day for Max too. He deserved a say in how we'd celebrate our nuptials.

"It makes no difference to me where we get married. All I want is to be able to call you my wife and for us all to have the same surname."

The gentle smile that crept onto Max's face told me that whatever made me happy would genuinely make him happy. He was always like that, wanting the best for our little family. Sometimes he went about things the wrong way, but it was always for the right reasons, and always with love. Me and Scarlett were lucky to have him.

We'd discussed surnames before, not long after finding out I was pregnant. Scarlett had been given a hyphenated name, which made sense to both of us seeing as she was half Max and half me. It had always been our plan that when we were finally married both Max and I would change names so we would all go by the surname Oakley-Drew.

Max's words reminded me of Norma's advice. It wasn't about the day, as easy as it was to get swept away with the excitement. Our wedding day was the start of our marriage, the first day of the rest of our lives. Looking at it in that context it was far easier to go for a lower-key occasion.

So long as we were married, nothing else mattered.

Our weekend visit to the woodland confirmed my instinct – I wanted a natural wedding without much fuss. The cool shaded glade was beautiful in its simplicity, and even Scarlett was fascinated as the shadows of the leaves cast twinkled dappled light over the forest floor. She was utterly mesmerised, her eyes open wide at the magical fairy tale setting. It was perfect.

Sadly neither of our families were as on board with the idea as we were.

Max's mum, Andrea, usually so bohemian in her outlook, had been the one person I'd expected to be in our corner. However, all she seemed to focus on was the fact that October in Newcastle is traditionally cold and wet. "Not ideal conditions for a woodland wedding. You'd catch your death of cold if it rained. Why don't you get married indoors and go to the woodlands after for photos?" she suggested. "You don't want the day being a complete washout."

But I knew what I had in mind. I'd never been the sort of girl who'd wanted the whole shebang, the enormous wedding with a full-on meringue dress and crystal tiara. Low-key and relaxed suited me just fine, as I politely but firmly told Andrea. The number of guests couldn't be cut back without offending anyone, but everything else could.

My parents were equally as unenthusiastic. "But remember how lovely Nick and Chantel's wedding was," Mum said. "Wouldn't you like a day like that? If money's the issue, me and your dad can help out. It's not every day our oldest child gets married."

Even though my parents weren't aware of the severity of the dire straits I'd got into financially, they had to have noticed a change in my lifestyle. Once my thirties hit I'd decided it was time to get my life in order. I had changed in so many ways. The external changes were the ones outsiders would notice, like my hair being a more natural shade (not to mention my skin no longer resembling a ripe tangerine), but it was the internal changes that had really shaped me.

As I'd chipped away at paying off my debts I'd learnt that possessions were not so important after all. I lived my life according to new rules, holding off on the rash purchases which would give me the quick high that for so many years had come from spending money, often money I didn't have. I'd come to appreciate the things that truly mattered to me, curating my belongings instead of filling my home with things I neither wanted nor needed.

"Nick and Chantel's wedding was beautiful," I agreed, looking at the photograph of my brother and his bride which was nestled at one corner of the sideboard. They'd had all the trimmings, no expense spared. "Perfect for them, but not for me and Max. We're not looking at the woods because we're poor, it's what we want. And I really appreciate you offering to contribute, but we're not planning on spending a fortune. We'd rather put money aside for Scarlett's future or for if something goes wrong with the house. Our roof's one of the only ones on the green that hasn't been redone. It wouldn't surprise me if winter finishes off some of the tiles that are hanging on for dear life. Having a roof over our heads, literally, is far more important than one overpriced day."

"If you're sure," Mum said slowly, before adding, "but I did get a pair of navy heels in the sale at Marilyn's boutique. Thought they'd be lovely for the wedding but I'm not sure I've got the balance to manage them in a forest. Not these days anyway, I'm out of practice. When I was younger I wore five-inch heels daily. My legs used to get a lot of compliments, didn't they, Bob?"

Dad nodded. "You always looked the part," he said fondly, and I was struck by the love in his tone.

"All right, all right, enough talk about Mum's legs," I said with a laugh. "We're supposed to be talking about me and Max's wedding."

"Sorry, Pumpkin," Mum mumbled, pulling a pot of lip balm out of her pocket before unscrewing the lid, circling her fingertip against the glistening solid and applying the shiny goo to her lips. "But I wasn't always old," she said pointedly. "I was quite a looker when I was younger, if I do say so myself."

"I can vouch for that," Dad chipped in, "I was the envy of Tyneside when I got with your mother. My mates all fancied her rotten but it was me she came home with."

"Anyway," I interjected loudly, to firmly bring the conversation to a close. "I didn't come to talk about that. Mum, I was hoping you'd come wedding dress shopping with me."

Colour flushed my mum's cheeks, the rosy blush of pride far more flattering than any make-up could ever be. Her eyes widened and I wondered if this was in a bid to hold back the swell of tears. "Are you sure you want me there? Wouldn't you rather go with Tawna and Eve? They know more about what's in fashion than I do."

"I was thinking they'd come along too, so we could pick out bridesmaids dresses."

I hoped my mum hadn't been expecting a one-on-one mother/daughter wedding dress shopping trip.

"I've managed to book appointments at two wedding shops next Saturday, so I'm hoping we'll find my ideal dress, and the perfect dresses for Tawna and Eve too."

The process of shopping for bridesmaids dresses for Tawna's wedding had been... let's say *trying*. Eve's straight-up-and-down figure was very different to the curves I'd been blessed with and finding something that suited us both was a challenge. I crossed my fingers for luck, because surely it wouldn't be as difficult to find a dress that worked for both my best friends.

Mum was more concerned about what I'd be wearing than Tawna and Eve's outfits.

"Are you sure it's a good idea getting the dress this soon? You've only just had a baby and you'll lose weight over the next few months, especially if you carry on breastfeeding."

"I'm sure I'm not the first new mum to have gone wedding dress shopping. People's weight fluctuates so much anyway. And lots of people are pregnant when they get married. I'm sure the staff must be used to dealing with all sorts of shapes and sizes."

My voice sounded haughty to my ears. For such a long time I'd battled my insecurities and Mum's comments had hit a nerve.

She knew I'd taken offence as she softly placed her hand on my arm.

"Don't take it to heart, pet. I didn't mean to upset you. You're my beautiful girl and I want you to feel your best on your big day. It'd be a shame for you to rush into getting a dress for it to be hanging off you."

"I think that's highly unlikely." All those biscuits had to go somewhere, and I reckoned ninety per cent of them went to my middle.

"You're so pretty, Sophie. You don't realise it, but you are. All me and your dad want is for you to have the wedding of your dreams."

"I will," I replied. "So long as I've got Max, I will."

CHAPTER 11

"We went to a lovely wedding last weekend, the son of someone Johnny knows," Tawna said vaguely, a faintly dismissive flick of her hand accompanying her comment. "I took tons of photos for you."

She pulled out her phone and brought up her camera roll, showing me images of a stunning couple outside a country manor house. It looked beautiful, but a million miles away from the kind of day me and Max would choose.

"Looks lovely. Where was it?"

"A hotel near Pickering. It rained all day but it didn't matter because it was one of those old houses with lots of nooks and crannies to hide in."

I laughed. "Why would you want to hide?" Tawna wasn't like me, if there was a party going on she'd be right at the heart of it.

My friend's eyes widened as she leant in ready to share a secret. "I didn't want to hide, but there was someone there who did…"

She paused, reaching for her mug of tea and taking a sip. Knowing Tawna, it was done purposefully, building up the drama. The silence was tantalising. Gossip was in short supply since having Scarlett, the news the new mums shared being far less scandalous than the stories I'd hear from my friends and workmates. Mia had confided she'd started weaning at sixteen weeks which had led to a debate between those who were trusting their instincts and those who were following the health visitors' advice to the letter.

"Go on. Don't leave me hanging."

It didn't matter that I wouldn't have the foggiest who she was talking about. A bit of vicarious excitement might be just what I needed.

"Darius was there with his new girlfriend. We hadn't met her before but Johnny says he's smitten."

"Oh." I didn't know how to respond. How was I supposed to react? Me and Darius were history, but there was a curiosity stirring inside me. "What's she like?"

Tawna placed down her mug. "Nice. Young."

"How young?"

"Twenty-two. She's just moved back up here after finishing her fashion degree."

Twenty-two. I could barely remember being that age. It felt like a different life.

"Why did they want to hide? Because of the age gap?"

Tawna shook her head, the glint of scandal twinkling in her eyes. "Apparently she used to date the groom."

I gawped. "No way."

"Yes way." Tawna laughed. "The bride had no idea she was there."

I was quietly horrified, trying to imagine how I'd feel if one of Max's exes turned up at our wedding. Then there was the strange feeling that I'd been replaced so quickly. It was only a year since Darius had been begging for me back, telling me I was the love of his life.

"And they got away with it?"

Tawna nodded. "Yeah. I guess everyone has secrets."

The conversation continued but my friend's comment touched a nerve. Scarlett had been less tetchy since our visit to Stonemont and I had a follow-up appointment booked, telling myself it was for her benefit.

The truth was, I hadn't been able to stop thinking of the emotions and urges Simon had brought to my surface. Sexuality, sensuality, desire. Pieces of me that had all but vanished since Scarlett's arrival.

CHAPTER 12

My plans to go wedding dress shopping didn't pan out as expected. The dreaded mastitis hit, turning my already heaving boobs into sore, swollen boulders. I wondered if it was punishment for the daydreams I'd been having about Simon and his magic hands.

Although mastitis had been mentioned in passing at antenatal classes, at the time I'd paid more attention to the session on giving birth and pain management options for during labour. When the midwife had spoken of inflamed breasts feeling like they were on fire I hadn't processed what that meant. Plus, an abstract idea was often very different from the actuality.

The reality was the fatty flesh turning an angry shade of purpley blue accompanied by a searing pain that made me want to claw at my skin. My temperature shot up and I was delusional with the pain, convinced Norma's Fred, who'd died the previous year, was standing in the corner of the room eulogising about Paul Gascoigne. Knowing Fred was a hallucination was a small crumb of comfort. My temperature was soaring and that, combined with lack of sleep, self-doubt, and the agonising throb of my breasts was almost too much to bear.

"This website says cabbage leaves can help." Max scrolled through his phone. "And keep taking painkillers to bring your temperature down. You'll need to make an appointment with the doctor tomorrow though, it's an infection so you'll need antibiotics."

"Have we got any cabbage in?" I asked, knowing the answer. Food shopping had been on my list of jobs to do for over a week, but it had fallen by the wayside and with wedding planning stepping up I hadn't got around to it. Being honest, cabbage wouldn't be the first item on my shopping list anyway, I'd be more likely to head for the freezer aisle to stock up on pizzas. We'd been running down the cupboards with Max resorting to visiting the corner shop on his way home from work to pick up bread and milk a couple of nights a week. Tea had been pasta in sauce for three nights in a row.

"I'll go and buy a cabbage, you can't go on like this. Anything's worth a try."

"Nowhere's going to be open at this time of night. I don't think the twenty-four-hour garage sells cabbage."

"I'll drive over to the big supermarket near your parents' house. I'm sure they're open twenty-four hours during the week."

"Pick up some more paracetamol when you're there?" I knew we were down to the last two tablets.

"Yep, and I'll take Scarlett with me, give you a break."

"I'm quite capable of looking after our daughter, thank you very much." It hurt that he felt it necessary to take Scarlett with him. Yes, I was in agony, it was as though I was being punished for having developed the curse of breastfeeding mothers.

"I know you are. You're more than capable, you're amazing. But that doesn't mean you don't need a break, especially when things aren't going your way. It says here expressing the milk will help bring your temperature down."

"At least I'll be able to build up the stores in the freezer," I said, glad there was at least one positive coming out of a lousy situation.

Max pulled a face, his teeth pressed tightly together. "You can't give it to Scarlett," he said apologetically. "It says here it's infected and giving it to her could make her poorly."

In that moment I could have swung for Google and knocked out whoever had posted the Wikipedia entry for mastitis.

"Well that's just great." Anger coursed through me. "As if this wasn't bad enough, now I can't even feed our daughter."

Max reached for his coat. "I'll pick up some formula milk as well."

"No," I shouted stubbornly. "There's milk I expressed in the freezer. We'll manage."

Max looked doubtful. "Is there enough to keep us going? If the doctor puts you on antibiotics it might be a while before you're able to feed again."

"There'll be enough," I snapped. "I haven't come this far to give up breastfeeding now."

Max picked up Scarlett from where she was lying on her play mat, and she gurgled her approval.

"Don't be too long," I begged, as a wave of pain rippled through my core.

"We'll be back as soon as we can," Max promised, planting a delicate butterfly kiss on my forehead. "And try hand expressing, it's meant to be helpful."

"All right," I replied grimly, although I felt so unwell I was willing to try almost anything. "I'll give it a go."

The door clicked closed and I was alone. I'd long since taken off my nursing bra, after the constraints of it caused me to wince in agony. With no one else around, I made my way to the kitchen, pulled down the blinds, and whipped off the loose-fitting top I'd been wearing. My breasts were enormous, rock hard and the colour of a glass of extra strong Ribena. Clenching my hands into fists I began massaging my left breast, the heat radiating from my body taking me by surprise.

I let out a gasp of relief as the watery milk spurted into the Belfast sink. I wanted to rid myself of the fluid, knowing that the less milk inside me the less pain I would be in.

Tears streamed down my face as I pummelled my chest. It didn't seem fair. After so long recovering from the birth, the stitches taking their sweet time to heal and the lochia which had meant relentless vaginal bleeding for three weeks solid, it was as though my whole being had been attacked. I squeezed and pressed and pummelled until my milk ducts were empty before moving on to my right breast. This was less painful, but the unpleasant throbbing sensation still caused my toes to curl in discomfort.

By the time my breasts were drained, I was exhausted. Heartbroken too, at the thought of all that wasted milk which could have been used to nurture our precious daughter.

I sat in silence, topless on the settee. It was only a matter of time before my body would produce more milk and the temporary relief would be replaced by the agonising burning.

Max and Scarlett seemed to have been gone for an age, and the house which I so loved was eerily silent in a way that houses can only be in the middle of the night. It was funny how I'd been desperate for peace and quiet for so long, but it was almost too still, somehow.

I didn't know what I wanted.

My mind wandered, moving from one random thought to another. Nothing seemed to make sense and that along with the pain and the soul-destroying tiredness only made me weep all the more.

That was how Max found me when he returned, a half-naked, crying shell of my usual self.

CHAPTER 13

*A*ll I wanted to do was sit perfectly still because as soon as I moved it was as though needles were being stuck into my chest.

Max, as ever, was lovely. Not only did he step up to the plate and takeover the day-to-day jobs in the house such as washing and ironing, he adjusted his working hours so he could come home at lunchtime and make sure that I ate a proper meal.

My appetite had gone too, which wasn't like me at all. For my whole life my appetite has never really waned.

Sadly, neither had Scarlett's. Reluctantly, I had to admit that Max was right and there wasn't enough frozen milk to nourish our daughter.

I cried as I made up the first bottle of formula milk, feeling yet again as though I'd failed.

Rachel, one of my mummy friends, rang me every day to see how I was doing, bless her. She was a huge support and adamant I didn't torment myself over my inability to breastfeed.

"I didn't breastfeed Millie at all, and she's turned out fine. She's top of her class in every subject. It's all well and good to breastfeed them if you can, but you don't need to beat yourself up if you can't."

Her words didn't reassure me. All I could think was that I hadn't reached my own high standards that I set as a mother.

"It was different for you," I said, "you were only a child yourself when you had Millie."

"Yeah, but it wasn't an option in my mind. I took the easy way out for everything," she paused, "or at least what I thought was the easy way out. I bottle fed, used disposable nappies, slept with her in the bed with me... I didn't have the headspace to think about my choices or their consequences. All I thought about was getting through each day."

Her words chimed with me. That was my aim; to survive, as if surviving was good enough. It wasn't though, because I had a vision of motherhood I couldn't live up to.

Before I knew it, I was sobbing my heart out down the line to my friend. My insecurities had escalated to a pressure point until there was nothing else for it – I had to let them burst out.

"I'm barely managing to get through each day at the moment. We're hardly getting any sleep and I'm so tired I can't think straight. Down below isn't sore but it still doesn't feel right and the painful tits make it hard to do anything. This whole mummy thing isn't what I expected."

My shoulders juddered as the uncomfortable words left my mouth, my hands quivering with the fear that Rachel would cast judgement.

I looked guiltily over to where Scarlett was sat in her bouncy chair. Was she going to be traumatised in later life after seeing me on the verge of a breakdown? A breakdown that her arrival played a major part in?

I wasn't being melodramatic. Emotionally and physically, I was a beaten woman. I'd known it for weeks.

Yet again I was doing the wrong thing.

"You've got to go easier on yourself," Rachel said firmly. "Parenthood isn't about being perfect, it's about doing your best."

"But what if my best isn't good enough? What then?"

The shaking hadn't stopped. If anything it had got worse.

"It will be," Rachel assured me. "You're struggling at the moment, but that's to be expected. Anyone would be finding it hard if they were going through what you are going through. You haven't had an easy ride. Another friend of mine had mastitis and said it was worse than labour. She went as far as begging her boyfriend to cut her breast off with a carving knife. You're stronger than you realise."

"I love Scarlett so much."

"Of course you do." Rachel's voice was a soothing balm. "Anyone can see how much you adore her. All you can do is your best at any given time. Your best today might not be the same as your best tomorrow or next week or next year. Motherhood doesn't happen in isolation from the rest of your life. It's a huge change, the biggest. And you're planning a wedding as well. Talk about trying to be Wonder Woman."

I laughed through my tears. I was a long way from being Wonder Woman.

"You need to give yourself more credit," my friend continued. "Beating yourself up won't do anyone any good. And you know we're all here to help you, Mia was asking about you, and I know Iris and Jessie would be cross if they thought you were struggling alone. You're one of the gang now, and that means sharing the load."

The kindness was almost too much to bear.

"I don't want people to think I can't cope."

"But why? It's normal to find things tough. That's why we need to support each other. The old saying about it taking a village to raise a child – well, it's true. With Millie, my parents had her during the week so I could stay at school, and I relied on their experience. I didn't have a clue about any of it before she arrived, why would I have? I was a teenage parent without any younger siblings, I didn't know the first thing about bringing up a baby."

"But I'm a thirty-one-year-old woman. I was finally getting my shit together, or so I thought. Turns out I'm no more a grown-up than I was before. I've been kidding myself all along."

"It's not about age. And asking for help doesn't make you a failure, it shows how strong you are, how self-aware. Please, promise me that when you're struggling you'll speak to one of us? You don't have to go through this alone."

I could detect the genuine concern in her tone.

"I'm not alone," I started, "Max has been amazing." I bit my tongue before I said something I might regret – that Max taking fatherhood in his stride, only compounded my self-doubt.

"Sometimes we're less honest with those we spend the most time with. I'm no psychologist, but I guess as humans we're wary about showing our weaknesses. Load of tosh if you ask me, there's no point letting things fester. It's far better to offload, and I'm always at the end of the phone if you want to talk."

"Thank you."

My chest swelled with gratitude (as well as mastitis).

"No problem," Rachel replied. "That's what friends are for."

&.

A course of antibiotics (along with the cabbage leaves) worked their magic although I was reluctant to mix with anyone due to the smell of sweaty, decomposing vegetable. It had a nasty habit of lingering on my skin long after removing the nobly green leaves. I was aware I smelt like the miniature compost bin that sits on the kitchen work surface but I didn't care. All that mattered was that the pain had gone and with it my ability to care for Scarlett returned.

The thought of feeding my daughter again rather than gently rubbing the wet tip of the latex bottle teat against her lips filled me with excitement. Breastfeeding was what I wanted, even with the toe-curling discomfort of latching on.

Scarlett, however, had other ideas. She'd forgotten how to feed, and as I offered the raspberry red nub of my nipple she had the gall to turn away from it.

"It'll come back to her, once she realises your gold top boob milk is on offer straight from the source," Max had encouraged.

The first night I'd felt confident. Perseverance and determination on my part would win out, I was sure of it. It had taken us both time to learn the skill first time around and all Scarlett needed was a few refresher sessions to get back into the swing of it. It'd be like riding a bike.

The following morning I had my doubts. She seemed far happier when she could snuggle with Daddy, rubbing her podgy cheeks against the brushed cotton of his T-shirt as he bottle fed.

I refused to be beaten, referring to online forums for tips from others who'd been in a similar situation. There was good advice but nothing seemed to trigger Scarlett's memory. I tried wearing the chunky breastfeeding necklace Tawna had given me, hoping it would captivate Scarlett long enough for her to latch on successfully. I tried dabbing milk around my areola and nipple hoping the taste would encourage her to suckle. On my health visitor's advice I tried rebirthing, a postnatal method of recreating the birth experience in a warm bath.

Every attempt was futile, and after two more weeks of forcing my breasts at Scarlett I eventually admitted defeat. I continued expressing, bags of milk filling up the chest freezer in the garage. The mastitis had given Scarlett a taste for formula so my own milk was out of favour.

Only when the option was taken away from me had I realised how bereft I was that our breastfeeding experience was over so soon after it had begun. I hadn't expected to feel such an enormous loss. It felt as if one thing after another was going wrong.

"What do the baby blues feel like?" I asked my health visitor, when I was teetering on the verge of tears yet again.

She explained, in a very matter of fact fashion, how the baby blues were a crash in the first week after birth which left new mothers feeling emotional.

I nodded along, unable to find the words to ask what it meant if I was still feeling emotional at this point. I didn't want to know the answer.

Of course, I didn't tell Max that the days seemed endless. He'd have loved to have been at home spending more time with Scarlett, so it would have been churlish of me to complain.

Instead I painted on a smile as he walked out of the door before standing at the window holding up Scarlett's hand to give her daddy a little wave as he climbed into the car. I watched as he reversed off the drive and turned onto the street, his trusty Mini pulling away. Only then would I allow myself to cry.

CHAPTER 14

I gathered my daughter right into my chest, sobbing into the grubby muslin square I used to mop up her dribble, drool and sick.

How had it come to this? Why did no one warn me that motherhood was like a race with one ginormous hurdle after another laid out ahead? Instead of gliding over the obstacles with ease I was crashing into them, hurting myself and looking like a prize idiot.

"Sophie! I miss you!" Tawna's familiar voice travelling down the line went some way to lifting my spirits. She was that kind of person, she wore her heart on her sleeve and I knew how difficult it must be for her to reach out to me when the one thing she wanted more than anything else in the world was a baby of her own. Even through my own self-pity I appreciated the effort she'd made. "How is my future god-daughter doing?"

"Bit presumptuous," I replied with a laugh. "Who said anything about you being godmother?"

"I'm the obvious choice. Eve loves Scarlett as much as I do but she's not the sort to take her out for manicures and pedicures, is she? Auntie Eve can be the one who helps with homework, but Auntie Tawna is the fun one and that's why I should be godmother. The whole point of the role is to be someone they can open up to without fear of being judged."

I thought of my own relationship with my godmothers. Auntie Trish was on the other side of the world, busy living out her dreams in sunny Sydney. She'd gone to Australia for a new start following her divorce and if her Facebook statuses were anything to go by she spent most of her time on the beach with her chocolate labradoodle, Gerald.

Norma was my other godmother and she really was someone I could talk to. Her common sense comments about the wedding had been helpful. Perhaps I could have been more honest with her about my parenting shortcomings too? She wouldn't judge me and as a mum herself she might be able to offer advice. Plus, she would be supportive, the way she always had been; reminding me how I was a tough cookie who never knew when she was beaten.

When looking back over my life I could recognise there were times it would have been easy to give up yet I never did; instead dusting myself off, picking myself up, and dealing with issues head on. That's what Norma always helped me see in myself, which in my opinion was the best gift a godmother could ever give.

"You could even have a double celebration. Wedding and christening in one." The enthusiasm in Tawna's tone suggested she was deadly serious. "Think about it, everyone you'd want there would be in the church already. And I know you're always looking for ways to get value for money. A joint do would mean one party instead of two."

"You know we're not going down the church route." Why did I sound apologetic? It was nothing to be ashamed of. Just because Tawna had gone for the traditional church wedding when she married Johnny, it didn't mean me and Max should do the same. "It would be different if we went every Sunday and were religious, but we're not."

"It doesn't have to be like that though," she said. I detected a pinch of defensiveness. "When we got married the vicar was over the moon to welcome us into the church. They weren't fussed about whether or not we went on Sundays."

Probably because the money Tawna and Johnny had paid for the use of the church and the cost of the bell ringers made it a lucrative Saturday. Not to mention that the floral arrangements had been gifted to the church after the ceremony. Whoever was responsible for the flower rota must have thought all their birthdays had come at once when they turned up to be greeted by the beautiful displays Tawna had commissioned.

"It's a nice idea." Diplomacy at its best. "It's just not very us."

There was a sigh, and then a pause before she finally spoke.

"No," she replied sadly, "I suppose it's not."

"I promise, mine and Max's wedding will be special in its own way. Anyway, enough of the wedding talk, tell me what's happening with you. Any progress on the flower course?"

She'd been toying with the idea of registering for the evening class for a while.

"I did it," she said, her voice brimming with pride. "I booked my place."

A squeal of delight came out of my mouth before I even realised. Tawna had been particularly lacking in direction for a long time. She didn't need to work, not when Johnny was such a successful businessman in the North East, but even Tawna, who liked the finer things in life, seemed to be tiring of the personal maintenance carousel. Pamper sessions were all well and good, but how fulfilling were they? What Tawna needed was a project and the floristry course sounded like it would fit the bill.

"I think you just perforated my ear drum." She laughed, but I could tell from the delight in her tone how excited she was about her new venture. "I really want to make a go of this, Soph. This could be the start of something amazing for me."

"You're going to smash it. I can tell by how enthusiastic you are every time you talk about floristry. With passion like that there's no way you can fail."

"I hope you're right. I'm feeling a bit nervous now. What if everyone else is a natural? I don't want it to be like back at school when I was the dunce and you and Eve were in the top set for everything."

"You were never a dunce. There were lots of things you were good at at school," I said generously.

Tawna's dirty laugh travelled down the line. "None of them got me a GCSE though, did they?"

I could imagine the glint in her eye. She had broken a few hearts when we were at school, that's for sure, moving from one boyfriend to the next faster than Usain Bolt runs the one hundred metres. Playing the field had continued until she met Johnny, when her "hump 'em and dump 'em" motto was quickly ditched and replaced by fidelity.

"Maybe not," I replied, laughing along with my friend. "But this will be different, you're interested in this. You're choosing to do it. It's not like at school where we had to do all those lessons we weren't bothered about."

Tawna let out a groan. "Those science lessons were the most boring thing I've ever sat through and totally pointless. I don't know how Eve went on to do it at A levels and university."

"It's just the way she is. She always worked as hard as she could. And now look at her she's promoted and writing all these important articles for journals. With you doing this floristry course too the pair of you put me to shame."

"You're doing the most important job of all. You're raising a tiny human being! And you're doing great."

From the other end of the line I could hear her swallowing

which made me wonder if she was thinking about how different things could have been for her and Johnny.

"You'll be doing it yourself soon enough, I'm sure of it," I replied. "And when you do you'll be doing a better job of it than I am. It takes all my willpower to build up the courage to leave the house. The outside world seems so big and scary now. It never used to be like that."

"It's only big and scary if you let it be. This is your city, your Newcastle. It's home. Why don't you see if Iris has any baby groups she can recommend? She might even come along with you. It'll do you and Scarlett good to socialise with other mums and babies. If Iris goes with you then you won't have to worry about walking into somewhere alone."

Tawna was trying to reassure me, I knew, but it was hard not to see it as yet another failure. Scarlett saw plenty of people, but I hadn't yet braved mother and toddler groups. I'd used the mastitis as an excuse to stay at home and slob about.

Enough was enough, I had to get a grip. It wasn't fair on Scarlett. She needed to see there were other little people like her. Was there an optimum time for introducing babies to other babies? What if I had left it too late and damaged my daughter's ability to form friendships with her peers? I wanted her to be confident enough to interact with people of her own age, especially as that was something I found difficult myself.

I knew what I had to do. After congratulating Tawna once more on taking the brave step to register for the college course, I politely ended the call and immediately phoned Iris. It was a terrifying thought but it was time to take Scarlett out into the big wide world.

CHAPTER 15

"Lindsay and Dexter?"

A red-headed lady with an equally red-headed child raised her hand. "Here."

"Lilac and Rory?"

The woman immediately to my left raised her hand. "Here."

"Iris and Dana?"

Iris, as always, was full of beans and confident in her new surroundings. As she smiled at the roomful of strangers I wished I could have half her confidence.

"That's us," she said, everyone smiling back at her, attracted by her friendliness. That's how it was with Iris, people were drawn to her, just the way I had been when I'd first met her at a baby sale.

"Georgina and Ronnie?"

Everyone looked around to see who'd respond. Even in our sleep deprived states we were eager to learn the names of the rest of the group.

When no response came, Alexandra, the baby massage leader, shrugged cheerfully.

"No sign? They might have been held up. I hear the traffic has been horrendous."

"There was an accident on the Belmont Road," chipped in an immaculately groomed lady with a baby dressed head to toe in baby Burberry. "Police closed the road, we were diverted through the industrial estate. I'm Sian, by the way," she said, raising her hand to wave, "and this is my little boy, Wade."

Compared to the rest of the group, Sian was polished. I suspected she spent plenty of time in the salon to get the footballer's wife look honed to perfection. Her skin was the same burnished amber as mine used to be, back in the days when spray tans and sun beds were regular appointments on my calendar.

Seeing her almost made me miss my former self. Sian looked great. Her eyebrows were impeccable which, along with her contouring make-up, gave her bone structure added definition. I wish I'd fully appreciated how much of a difference well-shaped brows make back when I had time to get them threaded. Since having Scarlett I'd not even had chance to pull out the most wayward hairs with tweezers.

My eyes kept wandering back to Sian and Wade, wondering how a new mum managed to pull off looking so good. She must have someone come to the house to do her treatments at home, because surely she couldn't be making regular trips to the salon with a newborn? Maybe she did, what did I know? Or perhaps she really was a WAG. If so, she'd have nannies and nurses to look after Wade while she kept on top of her beauty regime.

"Good to meet you, Sian," Alexandra said before turning to look in my direction. "Which means you must be Sophie and Scarlett?"

I nodded. "That's us."

"Wonderful. Then let's get started." She snapped shut the book she was using as a register, twisting her body to place it on the table behind her. "Has anyone here used baby massage before? Maybe with an older child?"

Alexandra looked around expectantly, only to be met with blank faces.

"I'll take that as a no then, shall I?" She laughed. "This is rather exciting. A class full of first-timers. Let me start by telling you a bit about me. I began using massage with my oldest daughter, Gracie, when she was a similar age to your children now. At first I made it up as I went along. She struggled with dreadful constipation as a baby which left her screaming in pain but I found rubbing her tummy eased her discomfort and calmed her down. It was like magic, and I struggled to find a class, so decided to train as a baby massage instructor to help other people who were going through what I'd gone through.

"That was twenty years ago and I've been teaching new mums everything I know ever since. You'll find the skills you learn over the next six weeks will calm your baby, help strengthen your bond and alleviate constipation, wind and other aches and pains."

She looked at each of the pairings wearing an encouraging smile. "Right, now I've introduced myself, let's get started. Firstly lay down your towels in front of you and strip your babies down until they're just wearing their nappies."

The babies were in various stages of undress when the doorbell rang.

"That's probably Georgina arriving," Alexandra said, excusing herself to answer the door.

During this time, Scarlett, unhappy at being undressed, decided it was the perfect opportunity to scream blue murder. I winced, waiting for the judging eyes to fall on me.

"Sorry, everybody," I mumbled. "She really doesn't like being cold."

"I don't blame her," Sian said, with a kind smile. "The only time I want to be near naked is when I'm lying on a sun lounger in a bikini with a sexy waiter keeping the cocktails coming all day long."

Scarlett wasn't the only baby who was less than impressed – Rory was also starting to complain as his mum wriggled him out of his sleepsuit; the first minor grumbles of an unsettled baby detectable even over Scarlett's ear-piercing cries.

Rory's mum smiled apologetically. "I don't know why I thought this would be a good idea. He usually naps around this time." Her mouth stretched in a yawn, her eyes blinking. "Most days I join him. He's a terrible sleeper."

Her honesty made me feel ever so slightly less alone. Scarlett still wiggled and wailed as I struggled to pull her vest over her head.

"I've got a tip for you," Iris whispered. "The slash-neck style is designed to pull downwards rather than over baby's head. Jude used to go ballistic every time we changed him so we found that pulling the Babygro down rather than over his head helped. I suppose it must be scary for them suddenly being plunged into darkness when they don't understand what's going on, especially when they're cold too."

I noticed the crossed-over flaps at the top of the vest did indeed slide down over Scarlett's shoulders. It was a far less stressful manoeuvre than trying to manipulate the cotton vest over her head.

"That's an amazing hack," I said gratefully, "a real game changer. Why isn't that something they teach you at the antenatal classes rather than other useless stuff?"

"I know, it's the best tip I've got. A baby shower I went to had a book to write down advice for the new mum and that was what I wrote. Hopefully it came in useful."

"I'd bet it did. If it's as simple as it was just now every time, it'll make changing times far less stressful."

Iris raised her eyebrows. "It was your baby shower, you doughnut."

"Oh," I replied, deadpan.

We burst out laughing as Alexandra walked back into the room along with a lady balancing a small child in her arms and a leopard-print changing bag on her shoulder. The strap was slipping and she cocked her shoulder to stop the bag falling to the floor.

The woman looked familiar, although I couldn't place where I knew her from. Had she served me in the supermarket or was she someone I went to school with? I knew lots of people in Newcastle, and even more by sight than I knew the names of. I tried to remember what Alexandra had said her name was... Jordan? Georgia? No, it was Georgina.

I wracked my brain trying to remember if I'd come across someone with that name but it wouldn't come to me.

"I'll give you two more minutes just to get settled and ready," Alexandra cooed. "And I'll put some relaxing music on in the background to help us get into the right frame of mind. The babies as well as the mums," she said with a smile.

She dimmed the lights and the dreaded sound of pan pipes began to fill the room. I've no idea who decided they were the perfect chill-out music, but whoever it was, I could have throttled them. Rather than helping me become the most Zen version of myself, my neck tensed up at the hollow sound. There's nothing relaxing about it. In fact I'd put money on that being the music that greets people at the gates of hell, either that or Gareth Gates.

I took a deep breath and tried to block the drone out as Alexandra demonstrated her massage skills and we all copied.

"Pour a small amount of olive oil into your palm and then rub your hands together to warm it," Alexandra instructed, demonstrating the motion. We'd each been given travel-sized bottles of olive oil to use, Alexandra informing us that it was better than fragranced alternatives due to babies having delicate skin. "Some essential oils are suitable for babies so you can always add a drop if you wanted to make it a multisensory experience. Lavender is, and can often help children who struggle to switch off to relax, and tea tree is great for unblocking snuffly noses."

We started by massaging the babies' arms. I pulled my hands gently down along the muscles in the repetitive motion.

Iris muttered, "This is exhausting. Is this what it's like being straight?"

I swallowed down my giggles as we moved on to massaging the legs using a similar method.

"That's great, Sian." Alexandra nodded her approval. "Look how calm Wade is now. He likes the contact." She turned her attention to Iris. "You can always add a little more oil if you need to. Your hands need to glide over baby's skin."

There was something quite relaxing about carrying out the rhythmic movements. It was nice too that the massage encouraged Scarlett to respond to my touch. She'd previously saved her smiles for Daddy but instead the corners of her lips turned up a fraction as I massaged her chubby limbs. It was a vote of confidence, a sign of love. It was also exactly what I needed to reassure me that it was worth making the effort.

I'd made the right choice. What Scarlett needed was new experiences, stimulation and time with people her own age. Truth be told, I needed exactly the same.

"Wonderful." Alexandra beamed at the group. "You're all getting the hang of it. Next we're going to move on to a stomach massage called the 'round the clock'. This is particularly good at aiding digestion and helping with any constipation or blockages. Don't worry if your child fills their nappy during this exercise.

It's quite normal for them to empty their bowels when there's pressure on their little stomachs."

Iris rolled her eyes. "What's the betting it'll be Dana who's filling her nappy?"

"It could just as easily be Scarlett. She hasn't done a poo since yesterday."

It was funny to think how my life had changed and poo was now a staple conversation in my repertoire. Not a talking point that everyone responds well to but still... there's limited news to share when you're busy bringing up a baby. It reminded me of when my sister-in-law, Chantel, had my nephew, Noah. She didn't talk about anything other than how many hours sleep she was getting and how she'd already put his name on the waiting list for the local nursery which had the best reputation.

I'd never said it out loud – I wouldn't dream of being rude to a family member – but in my head I thought she'd turned into a real baby bore. I loved Noah with all my heart and soul, but nobody else is as interested in a child as their parents, no matter how much they love them. Now I was one of the mummies I'd dismissed as having no life. How naïve I'd been.

I watched as Alexandra demonstrated how to perform the movement. It was circular and looked to me just like the stroking I did on my own stomach when I had belly ache after a dodgy Indian takeaway.

"Always clockwise," Alexandra reminded Lindsay. "That pushes everything around the bowel."

Checking out from the annoying pan pipes, I gave Scarlett my full attention, warming the oil between my palms ready to try out the new move. I was determined to make the most of this time to bond with my daughter. We had bonded already but it didn't seem to matter that she spent the majority of her time with me, she would still prefer to be with Max if she had the choice. I hoped this quality mother/daughter time would go some way to levelling the parenting playing field.

"Do you like that?" I purred and Scarlett gurgled happily in response. "Does that feel nice on your tummy?"

She had obviously relaxed and, as Alexandra had warned, a squelch that could only mean one thing came from her bottom end. Trust my daughter to be the first to poo.

Alexandra placed her hand on my shoulder as she stood behind me. "That shows you're doing it right. If you want to change her, the room next door has a changing table and wipes, nappy sacks, barrier cream... just let me know if there's anything you need."

"Thanks."

I lifted Scarlett, pulling her warm little body towards me and grabbed my changing bag. *At least it shouldn't take long because I haven't got to strip off all the clothes*, I thought.

By the time I returned, both Dana and Rory were also ready for changing. The aromatiser was doing its best to mask the smell, but instead the room had a fusty, musty scent of lavender mixed with poo that was reminiscent of the nursing home where my great aunt Sheila had lived out her last days.

"We have one more move to finish off the session, but I hope you'll all stay behind to chat and have a cup of tea and a slice of flapjack. It's the only thing I can make from scratch," she added apologetically. "I've tried my hand at cakes and biscuits, but there's either something wrong with me or with my oven because I always end up throwing them away. Flapjacks, I can manage."

We finished off our session and I pulled the soft pink fabric of Scarlett's vest over her head I heard Lilac talking to the girl who'd walked in, the one who looked so familiar. They were laughing about something, and whether it was the angle her chin was jutting out at or the gap between her two front teeth I don't know, but it was suddenly apparent to me where I'd seen her before. No wonder she hadn't recognised me, there was no reason for her to. She had no idea I existed, let alone who I was or, more significantly, who Scarlett was.

I could have kicked myself. She looked exactly the same as she had in the profile photo I'd seen on Facebook when I'd been snooping around in the early days of mine and Max's relationship.

Gina. Max's ex. The one who had vanished from his life and who I had the distinct impression he had never really got over.

CHAPTER 16

"That was good, wasn't it?"

Iris was wearing Dana in a sling and I was pushing Scarlett in the pram because I still hadn't mastered how to put a sling on single-handedly. I liked the idea but had tried all different sorts – some with clips and some which were more like long swathes of fabric that wrapped and twisted in a specific ways. Both had their merits but I still needed Max's help to ensure Scarlett was safely attached to my body. I was petrified that if I tried to do it myself the moment I let go of Scarlett the whole contraption would fall off my body. I had visions of Scarlett plummeting to the floor.

"It was all right."

My reply was non-committal. I'd been so happy throughout the session, loving having a purpose, learning a new skill and most of all spending time with other mums and babies. Until I'd realised Georgina was Gina – Max's Gina – I had been in my element, loving the baby massage group. I'd even come to terms with the dreaded pan pipes. Trust bloody Gina to rock up and spoil everything. Out of all the baby groups in all the world, she had to turn up at mine, didn't she? Talk about sod's law.

"Maybe we should try that playgroup at the church hall on Monday mornings? I've been before with Jude and it's all right. More for toddlers, really, but they have good biscuits. They do a music time at the end of each session with shakers. The little ones would probably like that bit."

"Maybe." I didn't want to make any promises, not when I was still rattled from having seen Gina at the baby massage class. What if she turned up at the church hall playgroup? Newcastle wasn't that big a place.

"Come on," Iris coaxed, "it'll get you out of the house. And now Jude's started going to nursery I've got no excuses for not doing all the baby groups with Dana. I do worry that she's missed out, there were so many things I did with Jude that I've not bothered doing this time around. Second child syndrome, I suppose. You'd be doing me a favour by coming along, it won't be any fun on my own."

She looked at me, her eyes pleading. Iris was very hard to say no to.

"All right, all right. We'll come along to keep you company. Happy now?"

"Yes!" She fist pumped the air like Sly Stallone at the end of one of the Rocky films. "It's exactly what we need. Let's try to enjoy it instead of seeing it as a chore."

"I would rather you come round for a coffee," I admitted. "It's exhausting meeting all these new people."

"You were pretty quiet," Iris noted. "They were a nice group and really easy to talk to. You should have joined in more."

My acting skills must have let me down yet again because I'd thought I had come across as chatty. I smiled in all the right places even though I was feeling discombobulated. I nodded along sagely when the other mums were talking about colic and debating when to start weaning.

Seeing Gina had shaken me, just when I was starting to build up my confidence.

Quietly, silently, I was dreading the next baby massage session.

CHAPTER 17

*L*ater that evening when me and Max sat down for our tea I still couldn't shake the awkward feelings that had been lingering since the baby massage class.

I didn't know what to do. Mention to Max that his ex had been sat across from me for the best part of an hour? The ex who had ghosted him and left him broken-hearted? Or keep it to myself and carry the weight of guilt on my shoulders?

I pushed a lump of mashed potato from one part of my plate to another without taking as much as a mouthful. A snail-trail of grease snaked across my plate where I was doing the same with my sausages. My stomach turned at the layer of fat coating the skin. Although I had not had an appetite to begin with, there certainly wasn't one after that.

"Are you sure you're okay? You normally love sausage and mash. I even made the gravy the way you like it, nice and thick."

Max was right; normally I'd be clamouring for second helpings of the creamy mashed potato. The finely chopped chives, fresh from the little herb garden that was forming on our kitchen windowsill, were a perfect garnish and an extra nob of butter melted into the potato for good measure added a mouthwatering richness. It looked delicious, but I couldn't even manage a mouthful. As if seeing Gina wasn't bad enough, she'd also stolen my appetite.

"I'm fine, just tired," I replied, before placing a forkful of potato into my mouth. The texture as it sat on my tongue made me want to gag. "It's been a long day."

"Oh yeah, today was the first of the baby massage sessions, wasn't it? How did it go?"

I swallowed the potato down in one choking lump.

"Fine."

Max was looking at me expectantly, waiting for me to elaborate.

"It was good. Like I expected, really. A group of mums and babies sat around in a circle following the instructor's lead."

That still wasn't enough information, I could tell. Max wanted the whole story not just the highlights.

I told him about the stomach massage and how it made three of the babies poo, about Wade in his designer outfit and even about the inane pan pipe music, which made Max laugh. I told him how Iris had asked me and Scarlett to join her at the playgroup. I told him about everything except for the one thing – or should that be the one person – who'd been playing on my mind ever since that morning.

"Brilliant. I'm glad you've agreed to give the playgroup a go too. It'll do you the world of good getting out of the house. I've been worried about you staying home so much, especially when I'm out at all day. You must be lonely."

"It's hard work getting Scarlett ready to leave the house." My shoulders automatically pulled upwards towards my ears in defence. "And without a car it's even more difficult because I can't face travelling on the bus, juggling bags and the pram and Scarlett and everything else. Iris gave me a lift today but I can't rely on her every time. It isn't fair dragging her all the way over here to pick me up. She's got enough on her plate dropping Jessie at work and Jude at nursery, and she's got Dana to get ready too. She doesn't want to be running around after me on top of all that."

"Maybe it's time you started driving lessons to give you more freedom?" Max suggested as he drove the sharp edge of his knife through his Cumberland sausage, stabbed it with a fork and brought the meat to his mouth. "There's only going to be more ferrying Scarlett around as she gets bigger. She'll be wanting to do swimming lessons and ballet classes and all the other things that her friends will be doing and we'll be the taxi service taking her here, there and everywhere."

An initial flicker of fear fluttered low in my tummy. I'd never been one of those people who wanted to learn to drive. Although I could see how it would offer more freedom, I couldn't imagine myself behind the wheel. The thought of being solely responsible for driving a car, a giant hunk of metal on wheels that travels at ridiculous speeds, filled me with dread. I was more than happy with Max ferrying me about and using public transport when he was at work. Or at least, I had been until Scarlett's arrival and all the worries that had come with it.

"You don't need to look so scared," Max said. "I'm sure you'd enjoy it once you got the hang of it. There are specialist driving instructors who help anxious drivers. I can see if Oz can recommend someone, he didn't learn to drive until a couple of years ago. Passed his test first time too, if I remember correctly."

"I never needed to drive before, when we lived down the road from the Metro route. That's the main problem with this place," I said, casting my hand around the room. "Now we're nowhere near the Metro and the buses only run once an hour."

"Even more reason for you to learn to drive. It's the perfect time. And I'd take you out in the car in the evening if you liked, give you a bit of extra practise. My mum would come and sit with Scarlett."

"I'm not sure..." I responded, although I was sure. I was sure I didn't want to learn to drive at any point in my life, and certainly not now when my confidence was at rock bottom and every little thing scared me half to death.

"Anyway," I said, purposefully changing the subject, "are we still going to your parents' tomorrow?"

Max nodded.

"We don't need to take anything. Belinda's making the cake and Mum's bought enough food to feed an army. I gave Grant some money towards a joint present and went and bought a card on my lunch break, so I think we're sorted." Max clicked his tongue. "Still can't get my head around my dad being seventy though."

"You're sure we don't need to take anything except ourselves?" The last thing I needed was Belinda being all high and mighty again.

"Nope, everyone was keen to make it as easy as possible for us 'cause they know how hard it is trying to do anything with a baby."

"Perfect." I lay my knife and fork in the four o'clock position. "Belinda's not going to start nagging about the wedding again, is she? Last time she gave me a headache going on and on. I'm surprised it didn't turn into a full-blown migraine."

"She means well."

"I know, but that doesn't make it any easier when she's forcing her opinions. Can you do something to distract her? And if you see her talking to me, come and tell me there's an emergency and you need my help."

Max laughed. "She's not that bad."

I pulled a face. "It's not you she's quizzing about the wedding."

"At least you've got an update for her now. We've got a date and a venue, you can tell her all about that. And I'm sure you'll revel in telling her you didn't have to book a venue a whole year in advance."

A smile worked its way onto my face. "There is that."

"We'll have a good time. It's a celebration." He leant down and kissed my forehead, a tingle radiating from the point his lips touched. "And I won't let Belinda harass you, I promise."

CHAPTER 18

The phone rang early the next morning, and because it was the house phone my day started with a tight chest and stress. The house phone is usually bad news, everyone rings our mobiles these days. I like that, as it means I can use caller ID and decide whether or not I should pick up. The house phone doesn't give that option.

Back in the old days, the pre-Scarlett days, I wouldn't have even been out of bed at seven on a Saturday morning. As it was I answered the phone to be met with Belinda hyperventilating down the line.

"You're going to have to help me, Sophie," she said, her voice an octave higher than its normal level. "The oven's on the blink and we can't get anyone out to fix it until Monday. Would you be able to rustle up a cake? It doesn't have to be anything amazing, a simple sponge will do. And I was going to put icing on the top that said '70 today'. Nothing too difficult, Hector won't mind what it looks like. But you can't have a birthday without a cake, can you? Blowing out the candles is part of the tradition."

Baking had never been my strength. I didn't even know if we had everything I'd need to make a cake in our cupboards.

"Sure."

Why had I agreed? Argh!

"You're a lifesaver. See you later, alligator."

"In a while, crocodile," I muttered to myself as I placed the handset back in its cradle.

No time like the present I thought, as Max was quite happy to get Scarlett changed and dressed.

Surprisingly I had all the ingredients necessary to make a simple sponge cake, even icing sugar (which was the one thing I thought I would need to run to the shop for).

Pulling up a foolproof recipe on my phone I set to work. I wasn't even sure why baking made me so nervous. It wasn't that I couldn't follow a recipe, because I wasn't that bad at preparing main meals, so long as I didn't have to rush. I'd just never mastered how to perfect the light and airy texture that seemed to come so easily to people who baked regularly. My mum, who loved baking, despaired of me. My efforts were either rock solid with an outer crust or didn't cook the whole way through and so when you cut into it the centre it was a sloppy mess.

Once the ingredients were weighed out and mixed together in the bowl I carefully tipped the mixture into the one and only cake tin I owned. It was heart shaped, from when I'd been with Darius and his daughter Summer had specifically requested a cake with a heart. It wasn't the most obvious choice for Hector, but it would have to do.

After checking the oven was preheated (twice – I'd made the mistake of forgetting to do that before and wasn't about to repeat that disaster) I carefully slid the metal tin onto the shelf. I looked at my watch and made a mental note of when to take it out of the oven.

I walked up the stairs filled with a quiet pride. The cake was in the oven and it was all going smoothly.

When I reached the bedroom Max and Scarlett were still

tucked up in bed. Scarlett was awake but not making a sound, her wide eyes studying the ceiling.

"Coming back in?" Max folded open the duvet and I couldn't resist. Lazy Saturday mornings were my favourite, so I happily slid under the cover to join my family.

I let out a sigh of contentment as he threw the cover back over me and snuggled up next to me.

Before long I had drifted off, back to dreamland.

🐚

I jolted awake in shock as the shrill pitch of the alarm rang throughout the house.

"What's going on? What's happening?" Max automatically reached for Scarlett and protectively drew her into his body. "I can smell burning."

That explained the relentless blast of the smoke alarm.

"Shit. Your dad's cake." I leapt out of bed and ran out of the room. "It must have burned," I called over my shoulder.

The sight that greeted me in the kitchen confirmed that the cake had indeed burned to a crisp. Smoke caught in my throat, bitter and thick, and the cake I'd been so confident about was completely black.

"Shit," I repeated, hopelessly throwing the window wide open as I wafted a takeaway flyer about in a bid to direct the smoke out of the kitchen. It was hard to breathe and I needed fresh air. "Shitting shitty shit."

The alarm was still going off and I looked frantically for something I could use to stop it before the neighbours complained.

When we'd moved in Max had been very thorough, ensuring the house had sufficient smoke and carbon monoxide alarms, but the place had ceilings which were high in the way that those in new build homes weren't. I wouldn't be able to reach them without a chair.

Max followed me into the room, armed with a sweeping brush that he used to turn off the blasted alarm, although echoes of the wailing continued to ring in my ears.

The baffled look on his face reminded me how I hadn't even told him about Belinda's panicked phone call and how I'd been called upon to save the day by baking Hector's birthday cake.

"What's going on?" He coughed.

"Belinda is having trouble with her oven. She rang first thing to ask me if I could help out by making your dad a cake. I must have forgotten to set the bloody timer and then I got back into bed with you and fell asleep. You should never have told me to get in."

"You can't blame me, I wouldn't have invited you back in if I'd known there was something in the oven."

Max pushed the window open further as well as propping the back door open, fanning a tea towel to help the air circulate and the smoke to leave the room.

The cake tin and the solid black mass inside it could go straight in the bin as soon as they had cooled down too. The tin was supposed to be non-stick, but I could tell from looking just how encrusted the cake was. No point in trying to scrub it clean. It was a goner.

"What are we going to do now? I used the last of the ingredients making that and in any case we're supposed to be there in two hours. Belinda's going to kill me. She says it can't be a birthday unless there's a cake with candles to blow out."

"Firstly, this is my dad we're talking about. He's not going to be bothered about candles so long as he's got a cold bottle of lager in his hand. Secondly, we can stop off on the way to buy one. We can always rely on Morrisons."

"Belinda said it has to have the number seventy on it," I

remembered, letting out a groan. "I'm never going to live this down, am I?"

"Don't stress about it. It's only a cake, hardly a matter of life or death. And Belinda can't say anything, she could quite easily have gone to the supermarket herself and bought one rather than ringing you first thing in the morning."

"You didn't hear Belinda, she's got a very specific idea about what she wants. She's going to go ballistic when she realises the cake isn't home-made."

Despite myself, I could feel the pressure building behind my eyes as the first tears of the day crept up on me.

"She'll get over it. You tried, even if you did almost burn the house down in the process."

Max put his arms around me and I pressed my nose into his T-shirt, inhaling the scent of his aftershave, the fabric conditioner and a night of sleep, but the dry smoky air was sticking in my throat and I could feel my chest tightening yet again. The dangers of the situation came sharply into focus and the thought that we could have been fast asleep as flames engulfed the house terrified me.

"You're shaking."

Max pulled back from me, his eyes connecting with mine.

"I'm okay," I lied.

"Look at your hands. They're quivering."

Until that point I thought I could control my emotions but once Max had pointed it out the shaking escalated.

"Hey, it's all right." The concern was apparent through his expression and he wrapped his arms around me once more in a comforting embrace. "We're all safe now."

The nervous energy I was becoming accustomed to carrying surged. Where was Scarlett? Why wasn't she here, her tiny body squished between us?

It was as though Max could read my mind. "Scarlett's

upstairs in the cot. She's fast asleep. I didn't want to bring her down until we'd got some air in, her lungs are only small so I thought she'd be better up there."

My heart continued pounding as I processed what Max was saying. A million "what ifs" raced through my head. What if the house had been razed to the ground? What if Max and I were asleep and died from smoke inhalation and Scarlett was left orphaned? What if the batteries had run out in the smoke alarm? Max rushing out to buy batteries for the system when we moved in had been part of the run-of-the-mill list of must-do jobs. Never had I expected it to be something that would potentially be saving our lives.

"You're still shaking. I'll get you a glass of water, help you calm down. Or something stronger?"

I shook my head. "Water's fine."

My hand was still trembling as he handed me the glass, the water sloshing over the rim of the cup and spilling onto my fingers.

"Sit down," he instructed, pulling out one of the stools from underneath the breakfast bar. "You're in shock."

The sip of chilled water brought with it a flash of clarity.

"Go and get Scarlett and take her outside." She was so small and the thought of the smoke clogging up her tiny lungs turned my anxieties up a notch. "Smoke rises, doesn't it? I'm sure that's what we were told at school. If it travels upstairs she won't be able to breathe."

Breathing was an effort for me too. The smoke-filled air didn't help but the clench in my chest went deeper than that.

As Max fetched Scarlett and took her outside the back door I allowed myself a moment to take stock. I knew I had to get a grip. I had to look as though I was coping, even if inside I was floundering wildly. Hector's party was fast approaching and no one could find out I was teetering so close to the brink.

CHAPTER 19

By the time we arrived at Max's parents' house I made sure that I was composed and calm. Instead of going to Morrisons, we had stopped off at Marks and Spencer's to collect a Caterpillar cake, which Max promised everyone would find amusing because he had always had one every year as he was growing up. I had concerns that one wasn't going to be big enough to serve everybody so, to be on the safe side, the very safe side, we bought three.

"It's so good to see you," Andrea said as we walked in to the Oakleys' back garden.

It was always a beautiful space but even more so with the decorations that signalled it was a special occasion. Bunting was strung between the trees, the triangular gingham flags waving happily in the breeze. Weighted helium balloons were placed on the table along with a large handmade sign that said "happy birthday grandad". It must have been Dylan's handiwork.

A long pasting table covered with colourful tablecloths and plates of nibbles had been set out along the patio; cling film tightly wrapped around the top of each plate to ensure none of the greenfly that Hector cursed for attacking his precious roses came into contact with the food.

"Hi, Mum. How're you doing?" Max gave his mum a squeeze and although it was obvious she loved him, her attention quickly moved on to her granddaughter.

"Fine, fine. And how's my lovely Scarlett today?" Andrea grinned. "You're getting bigger all the time, aren't you, sweetheart?"

"She really is. We had a clinic appointment on Monday and they said she's 10lbs 3oz now."

I'd worried how rapidly she should be gaining weight, after her slow start. The health visitor had reassured me that the move to formula would have contributed to this especially as now she was having bottles and we were aware of exactly how much milk she was having each day. Although that calmed my qualms about the rapid weight gain it did make me wonder if I'd been inadvertently starving Scarlett for the first weeks of her life. It was impossible not to think about how I may have been causing her growth to be stunted with my stubborn nature.

"It's so tiny really, isn't it? There's a lot of life for her to live before she's ready to be a big girl, but she's already changed over these past few weeks. She's looking more and more like you, Sophie. Don't you think?"

I shrugged. "Everyone else says she still looks like Max."

"Oh, we can tell he's the daddy," she laughed, "but look at her mouth and chin. It's almost exactly the same shape as yours."

I was quietly chuffed at this comment after so long hearing how Scarlett was a mini Max. Of course, I knew she was mine but it still made me feel strange to think that she was so much more like Max than like me. Everyone talks about children being a mix of their mums and dads but the barrage of people saying how like Max our daughter was had made me wonder about my own contribution to her genetic make-up. I didn't think it was a fifty-fifty split.

One by one Max's family members came over to see Scarlett. The comments they made filled me with pride.

"Look at how cute she is."

"Oh, isn't she a darling."

"A girl in the family at last. Our very own little princess."

Granddad Hector bagsied cuddles as he wore a too-tight T-shirt with "birthday boy" emblazoned across the front in large letters, a comedy present from Max's younger brother, Dale.

"I was going to get him a birthday tiara," Dale said with a wink, "but when I saw the T-shirt I thought it would be more suitable. Shame it's a slim-fit cut."

As Scarlett was merrily passed from person to person, I made the most of having my hands free. Angela had peeled back the cling film from the platters on the buffet and I filled my plate with a bit of everything – miniature pizzas, cheese and marmite rolls, and sausages on sticks.

"I was going to do a hedgehog as well," Andrea confided, "but I forgot to buy pineapple. Hector said I could have put cheese on the cocktail sticks with sausages but that wouldn't have been right." She rolled her eyes as though he was a fool. "A proper hedgehog has to be cheese and pineapple, don't you agree, Sophie?"

I nodded, my mouth full of hummus. Never mind that I didn't have a clue what she was going on about.

"I was going to dig out a photo of Max when he was little, so you could see what he looked like. He had these gorgeous little chubby cheeks," she smiled fondly, "and charmed everyone with his smile. He was such a happy little baby, he's always been good-natured. It was Grant who had the foul mood swings, and when he was a teenager..." she rolled her eyes, "let's just say we knew about it."

"I'd love to see Max's baby photos to compare him to Scarlett, especially as everyone says that they are so alike."

"All the albums are in the dresser in the dining room," Andrea said. "They won't miss us if we slide off for a bit. Come with me and we'll have a look."

I went to dispose of my plate on the table, but Andrea waved her hand. "Bring it with you. I know what it's like when you can't eat anything properly because you're holding the baby. Make the most of it. Fill your boots."

I followed Max's mum into the lounge and through into the connecting dining room. The dresser had drawers that were crammed full of photographs, some neatly stashed in albums and others still in the paper wallets they'd come in from the developers. Sadness washed over me as I realised all our photos of Scarlett were on our phones. I made a mental note that it would be a priority to print out photo books each month. She was changing so quickly and I didn't want to miss a moment.

As Andrea flicked open a book of photos, I was swamped by a deluge of packets of photos falling on top of me. Glossy rectangular images spilled out of their envelope packages, holiday snaps mixing with pictures of birthdays, graduations and new cars.

"Damn it. Serves me right for not putting them in their albums." Andrea tutted. "It's one of those things I keep saying I'll get round to doing but there's always something more pressing that takes priority."

She scooped up the photographs, shuffling them into envelopes willy-nilly, so I followed her lead. Most of the photos were recent, pictures of Dylan in his grey and yellow school uniform and even one of me and Max at one of the Oakleys' traditional Sunday gatherings.

My breath hitched as my eyes rested on a photograph of a family wedding. All the Oakley boys were there in their finery, arms around each other like a group of cancan girls lined up at the Moulin Rouge ready to perform a series of high kicks. First in line was Grant with his arm around Belinda, her other hand visible around Chris's waist. Chris's wife was next, dressed in her red and white spotty dress, long hair trailing over her shoulder. She was standing alongside Dale, mischievously poking his tongue out at the camera, and next to him was another face I knew. A face I'd seen recently.

Gina.

She was sideways on in the photo, eyes fixed firmly on Max who was stood to her left. But her profile was distinctive, her long chocolate brown hair tumbling in loose waves over her shoulders.

My hands tightened against the shiny photographic paper, the pressure of my grasp causing it to crumple. I didn't know how to react. Not that I was capable of making a conscious decision anyway when all that was running through my mind was a comparison of me, tired and covered in baby sick with roots that reached halfway down my scalp, and Gina, radiant in a silky floral sheath dress that screamed designer.

Everything about her was the antithesis of me in my current state. I tried to peel my eyes away but all I could see was the look her and Max were sharing in the photograph. The curl of her lips in a half smile made it look as though they were sharing a secret and from behind the lenses of Max's glasses I could detect the twinkle in his eye. They looked happy. And even though I knew that their relationship had not been perfect, not by a long shot, I couldn't help but feel that if Gina had stayed on the scene I wouldn't have had a look in.

Andrea, who was still busy collecting the photographs into piles, didn't notice how distracted I'd become, but unpleasant feelings bubbled inside me. Insecurity. Jealousy. And the deep and unsettling sadness that weighed heavy on my heart.

How was I going to be able to face Gina at baby massage after seeing this photo? My mind was racing at a million miles an hour and the enormity of the situation was becoming more apparent to me by the minute.

When I first realised it was her I'd been stung by the betrayal on Max's behalf, but having seen the photograph it wasn't only about Max anymore. It was about them as a couple. They had shared moments I knew nothing about, had made up their own silly little inside jokes I could never understand. They'd held hands, kissed, made love... Urgh. It was too much to take on board.

Max. My lovely Max.

But he wasn't just mine, I reminded myself, he had also been Gina's. Had he cared for her when she was poorly in the same way he took such good care of me when I myself was suffering with one of my regular crippling migraines? Had they been on trips to the same places we had, the same beaches, the same restaurants, the same Sunday barbecues in the Oakleys' garden? Had he gently nibbled her ear in the same way he nibbled mine when he was hinting at his arousal, the swell of his lips gently moving down from my earlobe to the underside of my chin to the soft flesh of my breasts. My stomach turned 180 degrees at the thought.

"Earth to Sophie." Andrea laughed as she waved her hand in front of my face. "You looked like you were miles away."

And how I wished I was.

CHAPTER 20

"*L*ook at that hair." Grant roared with laughter. "Talk about a bowl haircut."

"It's the matching jumpers that really make it. They finish off the look," Chris said with a chuckle. "What a mess."

Andrea feigned hurt, but there was a smile on her face too. "I knitted those sweaters especially for you three. Took me ages."

"Thank the Lord I missed out on that pleasure." Dale pressed his hands together as though in prayer, every inch the cheeky youngest child.

"Well, I think you all look very smart indeed," I interjected, always the diplomat. "Maybe you could do a recreation of it. I saw something on Facebook where a family had posed in the same places and clothes as in photos from their childhood and it was really sweet."

"I don't think so," Max said at the same time as Dale said, "I'd pay good money to see these three dressed up like that."

"There's no chance I'm making matching jumpers for you three now, it'd take me the best part of a year." Andrea beamed at her sons.

"We could always buy them instead. And get one for you too,

Dale. Wouldn't want you to feel like you were missing out." Hector let out a gruff laugh, as Bunty, the Oakley family's grumpy cat who hated everyone except Max's Dad, nuzzled against his legs before jumping into his lap and stealing a chunk of cheese from his paper plate.

"Ha bloody ha." Dale rolled his eyes but it was done with affection rather than disdain. "The one advantage of being the youngest is not being made to wear those hideous jumpers."

Grant snorted. "One advantage? You get away with murder, and you know it. And Mum and Dad were less strict by the time you came along. We were never allowed TVs in our rooms but you got a telly, PlayStation, the lot!"

"Different generation," Dale quipped, the cheeky expression of a youngest child spreading further across his face. "I can't help it that you lot are so much older."

"Now now, boys," Andrea interrupted, used to playing the role of referee between her sons. "You know we love you all equally."

Max draped his arm across his mum's shoulder, and Andrea rested her head against his chest. I still wasn't used to this touchy-feely aspect of family life. Hugs had been a part of my childhood, but not in the same way as it was in the Oakley family, where they were given at any opportunity.

"But Dale gets away with the most," my fiancé insisted. "Youngest sibling privileges."

The joking continued but I was distracted by the grumbles coming from Scarlett's direction. She'd been fed before we left but she'd been so hungry lately that I'd brought two bottles of milk with me just in case. When I'd mentioned my concerns to the health visitor, she'd not seemed fussed in the slightest, saying it could be a growth spurt and that babies know what they need so to allow Scarlett to take the lead. Which was all well and good, but exhausting, because it was nigh on impossible to plan anything.

"I'll take her," I said, hastily retrieving my daughter from my sister-in-law's arms before the noise got any louder. "She probably needs changing."

When I reached the upstairs room which had been Max's when he had lived at home, I lay her down on the bed, marvelling at the faces she pulled. The whines had stopped. Her enormous eyes – still blue, despite the warnings that they would probably change colour as she got older – were doll-like as she took in her surroundings, her lips pressed together in a pout.

"Hello, darling." I readjusted the hairband that had come as part of the clothes set I'd bought especially for the occasion. "Was it a bit noisy for you down there?"

I did the sniff-test, my nose getting very close to the silky over-nappy pants that matched the cherry-blossom pink party dress. All clear – no poopy aroma, nor the chemically nappy scent that accompanied a wee.

It was nice being away from all the noise, the clamour of family. Sometimes I wished both me and Max were only children, because family events were busy and there were so many of them. It was always someone's wedding anniversary, someone's birthday.

After I'd been in the room for twenty minutes' respite, I knew I'd have to rejoin the guests. There was only a limited time I'd be able to make excuses for, because everyone knew it didn't take long to change a nappy. Everyone except Dale, he probably didn't have a clue.

Part of the reason I was reluctant to go back into the garden was that the buffet was drawing to a close, which could only mean one thing – cake.

I hadn't mustered up the courage to tell Belinda about my earlier baking disaster, although I had given the caterpillar cakes to Andrea for safekeeping. She'd been amused by them, recalling how much Max had loved the cakes when he was younger.

"He always had the slice with the face, which was his prerogative as the birthday boy," she'd recalled. "And the other end, because it was the chocolatiest. His Dad'll get first dibs this time though."

Eventually, when I couldn't put it off any longer, I put on my metaphorical big girl pants and forced myself down the stairs and into the garden to join the others.

They all looked jolly, drinks in hand.

"Sophie, Sophie! You missed the cake," Max's nephew, Dylan, cried with dismay, chocolate smudged around his mouth. "It was a caterpillar one and tasted really yummy. Mine had a purple Smartie on it," he added proudly.

"She didn't miss it," Andrea corrected, handing me a side plate with a chocolatey ring on it. "She missed the singing, but that's not necessarily a bad thing. Your Uncle Dale's tone deaf," she said turning to Dylan, mimicking putting her hands over her ears. "I've heard more tuneful cats."

I glanced to see where Belinda was, waiting for her condescending comments about the cake coming from a shop. Please don't let it be a showdown in front of the whole family, I inwardly pleaded.

She was talking to Chris across the other side of the garden, her ever-loud voice explaining why one of the plants needed to be moved from the ground into a pot (something to do with needing lime in the soil, from what I could hear).

When she noticed me, she strode over and I braced myself for the onslaught. Her face was like thunder.

"I can't believe you did that with the cake. What a barefaced cheek." Her expression was stern and I could feel myself shrinking in response. Then, out of nowhere, she burst out laughing. "I'm only messing with you. You really showed me up though, the Colin Caterpillars were a masterstroke, everyone loves them."

It took me a moment to realise Belinda – clever clogs, know it all Belinda – wasn't angry.

"Thanks for making the detour to buy them too, I'll give you the cash seeing as it was my fault you needed to get the cake in the first place. Typical that my oven decided to play silly beggars, today of all days."

I was at a loss for words, but Belinda carried on talking at me.

The plate Andrea had given me was still in my hand, and I looked down at it mournfully. I was in desperate need of a sugar rush but with Scarlett in my arms it was impossible. Two hands weren't enough.

My future mother-in-law noticed my disappointment and held out her arms for her granddaughter.

"Come on, petal," she said, holding Scarlett at arms' length high above her head. "Come and have a cuddle with Grandma so Mummy can eat her cake."

I smiled gratefully, picking up the circular slice of cake. That was when I noticed it wasn't just any slice; I hadn't been able to tell before because it had been face down. As I turned the piece over I was met by the bright orange face of Colin the Caterpillar.

Looking up, I caught Andrea's eye and mouthed the words "thank you".

And in return, she gave me a knowing nod along with a wink.

CHAPTER 21

"Sorry for letting you down on Monday." Iris pulled an apologetic face as she looked over her shoulder to reverse out of my driveway. "I know you were really looking forward to the playgroup."

"Sarcasm doesn't suit you," I retorted, although sarcasm was as inbuilt in Iris as her Australian accent. "True, I wasn't exactly thrilled at the idea of going, but I would have come along to keep you company if Jude hadn't been sick."

Maybe. Although a tidal wave of relief had passed over me when I'd received the message from Iris bailing out. It meant I didn't have to come up with an excuse.

"He was really rough. Diarrhoea and vomiting have been going round the nursery so I guess he picked it up there. Those places are ripe for breeding germs. Not surprising when the kids have their fingers up their noses one minute and in their mouths the next."

"I'm just glad he's better, a poorly toddler can't be much fun."

"Oh, he's fine. It was a twenty-four-hour thing. He's just tired out from it now, and super grumpy." She looked both ways as she prepared to pull out of the junction. "Is Scarlett ready for baby massage? I swear Dana knew where we were going because she's been really chilled out all morning. Not that I'm complaining."

"She's not done a poo yet so I'm expecting the 'round the clock' to work its magic again." I laughed. "I brought three spare nappies with me, just in case."

"Now that's what I call prepared."

"Can't take any chances."

We made small talk for the rest of the journey, Iris filling me in on the gossip from our mutual mummy friends, before pulling up to park directly outside Alexandra's massage studio. Really it was her house, a nice but run-of-the-mill three-bedroomed terrace with one room dedicated to baby massage, but the website proudly proclaimed it as a studio. Who was I to piss on Alexandra's bonfire?

"You look different." Iris squinted at me from one back door of the car to the other as we unbuckled the car seats. "I can't put my finger on what it is. New clothes?"

I shook my head, running my hand over the navy and white striped hoodie I'd picked up from a car boot sale the previous year. "This old thing? Nah."

My friend frowned as she studied me, before exclaiming, "I know what it is, you're wearing make-up."

Rumbled.

The look I'd been going for was a natural everyday look, and I started to doubt I'd fulfilled my own brief. So much for looking like myself but better, if Iris had noticed, the other mums at the class were going to wonder how I'd had a glow-up in just seven days.

"Only a touch. The bags under my eyes were getting worse so I put on a bit of concealer to cover them up."

The concealer had led to me applying a full face, all in

neutral pinks and browns, but obviously not neutral enough to go unnoticed.

"You look great." Iris smiled at me approvingly. "You'll put the rest of us to shame."

"Not Sian," I replied, recalling her flawless but not so natural appearance. "I don't get the impression she's the 'roll out of bed and take me as you find me' type."

"Probably not," Iris agreed amiably. "But the rest of them will be throwing you daggers. You, Sophie Drew, are one yummy mummy."

I smiled to myself. Making the rest of the group jealous wasn't on my agenda, but feeling good about my own appearance had been a prerequisite of me going to baby massage that morning.

If I was going to spend an hour in the same room as Max's ex, I needed my war paint.

The second massage session was easier, Alexandra not needing to explain in as much depth meaning there was more hands-on time for mummies and babies. In place of the torturous pan pipes was a relaxing piano piece. In fact, I would have been pretty blissed out if it hadn't been for Gina being directly opposite.

However hard I tried, I couldn't avoid looking at her. Even when I channelled all my energy into focusing on Scarlett, Gina's hand movements would distract me, creeping into the corner of my eye line whether I wanted her to or not.

She smiled at me a few times, flashing the gap between her teeth and crinkling up her nose in a way that should have made her look ugly but was actually cute. I had to begrudgingly admit she was attractive. No wonder Max had been so besotted with her.

The confidence I'd had earlier that day when I'd been taking in my improved appearance dissipated. A bit of make-up wasn't going to help me out. Gina's good looks were genetic, not painted on.

When the session was over, Alexandra turned from massage instructor to tea hostess, bringing out her oat and raisin flapjack. That was my cue to hide in the toilet, I'd been able to bury my emotions when I'd been busy but didn't know if I'd have the strength to do the same when everyone was making idle chit chat.

The trouble with the babies all being in nappies was that it was obvious Scarlett's nappy was dry. Even the poo-inducing massage had failed me. Drastic measures were needed, so it was time to tell Iris a little white lie (okay, a big whopping lie).

"I'm not feeling so good." I bent double and clutched my stomach. "Can we leave early?"

Iris sighed, and for a moment I thought she was going to say no. "Don't say you've caught this bug now. This is exactly how Jude started, hunched over like our friend at Notre Dame. An hour later he was chucking up carrots."

So much for pretending to be ill, the image was enough to bring the taste of vomit to my mouth.

I clamped my lips together and gagged.

That was the clincher. Iris picked up Dana and her rucksack and we swiftly said our goodbyes to the rest of the group.

I was purposefully silent on the journey back. Iris was quiet too.

And when she dropped me and Scarlett off, with instructions to go to bed and rest, I didn't argue. Hiding under the covers away from the realities of life was a very, very appealing prospect.

CHAPTER 22

Sometimes all it takes to feel better is a few days of rest and retreat.

This wasn't one of those times.

Actually, that's not completely true. I was marginally better, as well as disgusted with myself, which was why I made a conscious effort to feel the best I could. Make-up and clothes are superficial, but it's hard to feel good about yourself when you haven't washed your hair for a week and your jumper has a ketchup stain down the front of it.

Getting up earlier sounded torturous, but I was determined. I set an alarm, for an hour before Scarlett's usual wake up time, with the intent to shower, wash my hair, apply make-up and put on clothes that didn't have an elasticated waist.

The first morning didn't go to plan, when instead of getting out of bed I pressed snooze three times. When I did get out to start the day it was because Scarlett was crying, ready for her early morning feed.

The second day wasn't much better, with Max needing to be in work early so hogging the shower.

Third time was a charm though, with Scarlett staying fast

asleep as I enjoyed a long shower. The stream of warm water drizzling down my body was relaxing and I was able to appreciate the shower gel Eve had given me in the "new mum" basket she'd put together. The scent was amazing; fresh and clean and reminiscent of the countryside. It was exactly what I needed to wake me up and I even found myself singing my happy song, One Direction's "What Makes You Beautiful".

After drying myself with a super soft fluffy towel I slathered the matching body lotion over my skin. Funny how something I had taken for granted felt like such a luxury.

It was wonderful to feel so clean. Showers had become something to squeeze into my busy day, more a chore than a pleasure. This was different. Me time, and much needed me time at that.

Next I dried and straightened my hair, before applying a foundation to my skin. Blusher, lipstick, eyeshadow and liner and mascara brightened my face, enhancing my features. My reflection stared back at me from the mirror and rather than the sinking feeling I'd come to expect I was quietly pleased with my more polished appearance. I stood looking at myself for a good five minutes. Not bad for a new mum, I thought.

I spritzed perfume onto my wrists, dabbed it onto my neck and even added a squirt to the back of my knees, a tip I'd heard somewhere long ago.

The outfit I'd laid out on the chair in our bedroom was ironed – a denim button-down pinafore, long-sleeved floral top and, in the ultimate bid to make an effort, pulled on a pair of mustard tights I'd bought on a whim in Primark.

Not bad, Soph. Not bad at all.

As Scarlett decided a lie-in was in order I happily made me and Max bacon and egg butties.

My fiancé wolf whistled as he entered the kitchen. "What are we celebrating?" I could see the cogs in his brain whirring, probably wondering if it was the anniversary of us getting together or some other event that needed marking.

"Nothing in particular," I replied in a singsong voice, wriggling a fried egg onto the stainless-steel fish slice before placing it on the bread roll. "Just life. Thought I'd make an effort."

"I'm not complaining, you look gorgeous. And I love the tights. Very funky."

I performed a little twirl as I handed him his breakfast before bending into a curtsy. "Thank you."

The peace didn't last long, with Scarlett ready to start the day seconds after I'd taken the first bite of my buttie.

Even so, I was ready to bring my A-game. It was going to be a good day, I could tell.

*

"Damn."

There's not much more frustrating than reaching the fridge to find there's no milk, or – and this is almost worse – the tiniest splash left in the bottom of the bottle.

I'd already put the teabag and the water into my mug (team Tiffie rather than Miffie – can't be doing with milk in first) but no way was I going to stoop so low as to drink black tea. A girl has standards.

Empowered by my early morning pamper session, I made the decision to be brave and take Scarlett to the supermarket. Getting ready was the usual rigmarole of changing bags and making sure the sunshield was attached to the pram but I stepped out with a smile and didn't even feel self-conscious as the neighbours stopped to fuss over Scarlett as I made my way across the green.

Everything was wonderful, the sky overhead bright and cloudless, as me and my daughter took on the world.

When we reached the corner shop my confidence was brimming over. Yes, I was tired, but we were out and about and I was doing an everyday task without feeling as though it was a mountainous effort.

Armed with a new lease of life, I decided it was time for a new challenge. I couldn't stay home forever and I'd have to get over my fear of taking Scarlett on the bus.

There were undeniable butterflies in my stomach as we waited at the bus stop and I found myself nervously drumming my fingers against the pram's handlebars. Typically, the bus was five minutes late, but when it arrived the driver was an absolute gem, leaving his cab to lift the pram from the path to the bus.

The city whizzed by through the window, streets I'd been down so many times before being viewed with new eyes.

I'd already made my mind up to go and visit Max at the charity shop, knowing full well he'd be surprised to see us in the centre of town.

I was right.

"What are you doing here?" His jaw was slack with surprise. "My gorgeous girls."

He called over the elder gentleman volunteer to meet us, introducing me as his fiancée, which still gave me a warm glow inside.

I browsed the racks as Scarlett enjoyed a cuddle with Daddy, finding a pretty pair of lemon-yellow dungarees for Scarlett and a black corduroy skirt for me, the tags attached to it telling me it had never been worn.

After I'd bought the items we – me and Scarlett, with Max having to stay at work – moved on to a café for brunch. It all felt very dignified as I sliced through my pain au chocolat and sipped on a delicious strong coffee. I could get used to this.

We mooched around town for a while longer, browsing in a few of the shops and looking at people who passed us on the pavement. It was a release. It felt normal.

A strange wave of nostalgia hit me and I had a sudden longing to head towards the quayside. So many drunken nights had been spent in the bars that lined the river. It felt like a lifetime ago that me, Tawna and Eve had been downing tequila slammers and busting moves on the dance floor. It was almost hard to believe it happened to me, because it was so far removed from my life these past few months.

The view over the river still made my heart full. Other people might rave about Paris or London, but in my eyes nothing would ever beat Newcastle. We had an unbreakable connection. It was, and would always be, home. It was beautiful in its own way.

I found a bench to sit on and rest, taking in the view. Squawks of seagulls filled the air and as I looked over to the opposite bank and the armadillo like Sage building in Gateshead I felt blessed to have been born here. I'd been brought up in an area where everyone was friendly and had managed to keep a real sense of community even in the twenty-first century. Friends had been made at football, at school, at the many bars I'd frequented. There was nothing better than feeling part of something. I hoped Scarlett would have the same joy and love for the amazing city we lived in.

Eventually, after giving Scarlett a bottle, I reluctantly moved from the spot. Scarlett would be ready for a nap soon and it would be better for her, and for me, if that was at home.

As I walked through the city my cheeks hurt from smiling so much, from the knowledge the old Sophie hadn't completely disappeared. She was still there deep down, mummyhood just one part of her.

Blissfully daydreamy, I headed towards the bus station in the centre of town. It did mean pushing the pram uphill but nothing was going to dampen my spirits. With my new-found positive outlook I told myself it was building up my biceps. Who needed a gym?

That was until I stepped into the road to be greeted by screech of brakes and a long drawn-out honk of a car horn.

A black Jeep had stopped just millimetres away from us, the bumper almost touching the mustard nylon of my tights. Scarlett, unaware, lay dozily in her pram but shock coursed through me and I was fixed to the spot with fear.

An angry red-faced man stormed out of the driver's side of the car. "What the hell do you think you're playing at stepping out in the road like that? Look where you're bloody well going."

The shock of the situation had me frozen and mute.

"And you with a baby and all," he continued, his voice loudening. "You need to open your eyes. What kind of person steps out without even looking?"

"I-I-I...," I started, unable to formulate a coherent sentence.

"I-I-I," he mimicked cruelly. "Just get off the road. You don't even deserve to be a mother, you can't look after yourself let alone take care of the baby." He shook his head, a look of disgust on his face. "And what are those tights all about? You look ridiculous. Who do you think you are? Marge bloody Simpson?"

Somehow, from somewhere, I found the strength to make my way onto the safety of the pavement.

I heard the slam of the car door and the rev of the Jeep's engine. As he left, there was one parting shot.

"You're gonna get yourself killed, you stupid woman."

He roared off, leaving me shaking. I couldn't believe I'd taken such a risk by bringing Scarlett into such a dangerous situation. What had I been thinking bringing her into the city centre? There were cars and people off their heads on drugs. It wasn't like being on our road where the biggest scandal had been the theft of six bottles of Riesling from Carla across the road's shed.

How long I stood there, I couldn't say. My hands gripped the pram trying to make up for my earlier carelessness.

I tried to remember the yoga breathing for relaxation, but it had been a long time since I'd been able to practise. I forced myself to move, timing my steps to coincide with the structured breathing.

My legs seemed to carry me without my brain engaging and I walked dazed through the streets.

I hadn't realised where I'd been heading until I found myself on the Tyne Bridge, staring down into the murky brown water of the river below.

My mind was swimming with thoughts of what it would be like to jump off as the wind blew through my straightened hair. Of free-falling before breaking the surface of the water with my body. What it would be like to sink down, down, down onto the riverbed to sleep for all eternity with the silt and rubbish that lined it. Would it hurt as I pierced the water? Would I gasp and gulp as I sank, the filth of the river filling my lungs? Would I be aware of anything as my senses shutdown and the world turned black?

It sounded appealing. There was only one thing stopping me, the little girl babbling away in her pram with no idea how hopeless her mother felt. Instead I slipped out of my shoes and, in full view of the cars leaving and entering the city, ripped off my tights and threw them over the edge of the iconic bridge.

A wail came from within me, desperate and animalistic.

Then I turned round and walked back towards the city centre. Only once did I look longingly over my shoulder and down into the depths of the Tyne, trying to catch a glimpse of my dusky yellow tights succumbing to the water.

AUGUST

CHAPTER 23

Wedding planning continued in earnest. It had to, as the big day was drawing ever closer. Having Tawna, the queen of organisation, on my team was a help and a hindrance. She knew exactly what to prioritise and on the days when I wasn't in the mood for tackling any of the items on the list she made sure I got my bum in gear and did something, however small.

Dress shopping was pencilled in and we'd arranged to hire a lovely converted barn and the surrounding grounds for the evening reception, all within a five-minute drive of the woodland where Max and I were going to exchange our vows.

To the outside world it looked as though I was in control. I worked hard at maintaining a cheery tone and a smile, although inside I was spiralling. The lack of shut-eye was taking its toll and every morning I'd wake up feeling sure I'd not had a minute of sleep.

Sundays – which I'd previously loved because of the family time it signalled – were the worst. The morning was usually fine, but as soon as lunchtime rolled around I'd start to panic, partly about Max being back at work the following day and partly

127

dreading the next day's baby massage class because I'd have to face Gina.

"Are you sure there's nothing you need me to do for the wedding?" Max asked, time and time again. "I want to share the load. You seem so tired and dazed lately."

I'd replied that I was fine, that it was normal for a new mum to be tired. Everything was in hand and there was nothing he needed to do other than get fitted for his suit. Bullshit, bullshit, bullshit.

With every passing week the weight of knowing Gina was in Newcastle seemed to get heavier. I wished I'd told Max she was in the same baby massage class as soon as I'd realised it was her because too much time had passed and now it felt like a dirty secret.

I convinced myself that if he knew where she was, he would leave me and Scarlett. My brain was telling me he'd be furious that I'd kept her whereabouts a secret. The whole situation was one great big worry-inducing mess.

The final straw came on the bank holiday weekend, which coincided with Max's birthday. Rather than a party we had an open house and friends and family dropped in throughout the day. In the evening he had arranged to go to the pub with his good friends Iain, Oz and Archie. Eve, who I hadn't seen for weeks, came over to keep me company.

Scarlett, worn out from all the attention the visitors had lavished on her, was sound asleep by the time Eve arrived.

My friend had barely had chance to say hello before I unravelled.

"Everyone I love hates me."

Salty tears fell freely, slithering down my cheeks and landing on my lips, all except one over-achiever that traced my jawline before sliding down my neck and landing in the dip at my throat. The sensation left me feeling more vulnerable than ever but I lacked the strength to even try to hold them in. "I didn't know it was possible to be super-needy but push everyone away at the same time," I sobbed, "but that's what I'm doing. I'm shit at adulting. I'm an awful friend, a useless mum, a waste of space as a partner…"

"Stop it," Eve instructed, her voice firm but not harsh. "You're being far too hard on yourself."

"But it's true," I said, the self-doubt swelling within me. It was like nightfall in winter, a sudden and all-consuming darkness. "I can't do anything right."

It was hard admitting my feelings to anyone, even my oldest friend. Far easier just to push everyone away rather than face up to my failings in every aspect of my life.

"Let's talk about this over a coffee," Eve said, calmly taking charge of the situation by switching on the Tassimo and making us both a drink.

I took a sip of the coffee, savouring the creamy texture on my tongue, coating my throat before the bitter aftertaste hit, along with the guilt. Caffeine. Shit. I was trying not to drink coffee while I was still expressing.

"Soph," Eve warned, dragging the single syllable out. "You're tired. This was always going to be difficult. You've got a tiny baby and you're not leaving the house if you can get out of it. You're not letting us in, and Max is busy at work and not around to help you out."

My stomach lurched. This week had been the toughest yet and when Max had left for work on Monday morning I'd longed to run after him. I didn't know how I'd get through another week of looking after Scarlett alone. Every time she looked up at me, her blue eyes wide and expectant, panic took over. She was so tiny, barely the length of my forearm and as light as the proverbial feather. And it was all down to me to keep her happy and safe and ALIVE. How did people do this every day and not go doolally when I was only three months into parenthood and losing my mind?

"You'll find your feet once you settle into your new routine," my friend assured me. "I bet if you ask your mummy friends they'll say they felt the same at this stage. The mood swings I get each month from PMT are bad enough so I can't even begin to imagine what it's like for you. Your hormones must be all over the place."

"It's not my hormones," I barked. "I don't believe in hormones."

"Well, you can not believe in them all you want, but I can guarantee they exist." That was typical of Eve, throwing science in my face. Sometimes I wish she was less of a brainbox. Maybe I picked the wrong friend to offload to. You wouldn't catch Tawna quoting science journals. You wouldn't catch Tawna quoting anything. Other than the glossy mags she devoured on her weekly trips to the hair salon the third member of our tribe never read a thing. "And you've just had a baby for crying out loud. Your body's gone through a trauma."

I laughed through my tears at that. It certainly had. I barely recognised the body I was living in as my own anymore. The skin around my stomach, stretched so taut during the later stages of my pregnancy when Scarlett was a solid bundle in my womb, was as squidgy as a lump of play dough. And my boobs? They'd always been big, but since Scarlett they were practically pornographic – two rock hard breasts full of milk covered with an ugly roadmap of blue veins. They ached too, a dull weighty ache that made me pity dairy cows and their engorged udders.

"It's a trauma all right," I said, remembering the terrible days of mastitis when I'd spent hours readjusting the cabbage leaf down my bra so the shell-like curve cupped my raging boobs. "I've had stitches in my fanny, cracked nipples and it's fair to say

I never imagined the day would come where I'd be glad to have leafy veg shoved in my undies. What's happened to my life?"

"You've become a mum," Eve said gently, before lowering onto her haunches next to a photo of Scarlett in hospital on the day she was born. My daughter looked miniature in the shot – she'd long since lost the look of a fresh from the womb newborn. "And look at what you made! Scarlett's the most beautiful baby in all the world." Eve reached out and gently stroked the photo and I could tell she was imagining the back of her hand was running along the velvet soft skin of Scarlett's cheek rather than the cool glass of the frame. "Her Auntie Eve loves her to bits."

"She loves you too."

Bless Eve and her kind heart. She's such a caring person by nature, born to nurture others, just like her mum had before her. Eve's personable way is why Tawna finds it hard to accept that our friend's happy being on her own; but after the initial blip when she first moved into her new flat, reluctantly leaving the house she'd grown up in so the money from the sale could fund her mum's care, she was loving having her own space.

"Please don't beat yourself up, Soph." The face she pulled was so sad, lips pressed into a wibbly line, her eyebrows lowered in concern. "You're a first-time mum, you can't expect to find it easy."

"But I read all the books, went to the classes, listened to everyone's advice. I should know what I'm doing."

"I think parenthood's one of those things in life nothing can prepare you for. You're doing brilliantly, I promise you."

I felt my right breast leaking, and reluctantly reached for the breast pump. Exhaustion coursed through me and the thought of even moving my hand made me feel tireder still. I pulled up my top, lowered the cup of my bra and unleashed the beast. Time to express.

Eve winced.

"I know it looks awful," I said, clamping the plastic funnel over my nipple. Even that was uncomfortable. A dribble of off-white milk escaped in response. I squeezed the white handle and pulled a face. It wasn't as painful as it had been when trying to get Scarlett properly latched on, which was toe-curlingly awful, but it was still uncomfortable. "I told Max I don't know if I can carry on expressing much longer, but he thinks I should even though Scarlett prefers formula. The midwife said the same. If one more person tells me 'breast is best' I might scream."

"I'm no expert but I'd say whatever makes life more bearable is best," Eve said wisely.

"That's easy to say when it's not you being ambushed by everyone. It's all boobs, boobs, boobs. At the baby groups the mums make it look so easy. Then on the telly it's all these Mother Earth types in some state of bonding bliss." I inadvertently flinched as memories of Scarlett suckling at my engorged red nipples passed before my eyes. "Why couldn't I do it, Eve? What's wrong with me?"

A sympathetic sigh escaped my friend's lips. "There's nothing wrong with you. Anyone can see you persevered and persevered."

"It's not enough though, is it?" My trigger-happy thumb click-click-clicked away, the squeaky mechanism a steady hum in the background. "I failed Scarlett right at the start. I couldn't even feed her myself. No wonder she prefers Max to me."

The wallowing was kind of cathartic. Trying to keep going all the time, painting on a smile to mask the complete and utter exhaustion that was now as much a part of me as my straw-blonde hair and my love of crafts, wasn't helping my mental state. Offloading on Eve was nothing new – I'd been doing it ever since we were eleven-year-olds. Back then my complaints were focused on my lack of boobs rather than how they functioned. Funny how things change.

"Have you told Max how you're feeling?" Eve's dark eyebrows were furrowed in concern, only separated by the most faint crease – possibly even the beginning of a wrinkle.

I shook my head sadly, the sting of tears burning my eyes. "How can I? We've got a beautiful daughter, a gorgeous house, a wedding on the horizon... what have I got to complain about? These are supposed to be some of the happiest times of my life."

Eve placed her hand on my arm, giving it a soft squeeze of comfort. "I'm worried about you. Tawna is too." Eve took a deep breath before speaking again. "Have you considered that you might have postnatal depression?"

Her eyes bored into me, her words hitting me like a punch. Everyone had the baby blues, didn't they? Mum had, and Mia. Wasn't it normal to love your child but mourn for the life you had before? The person you were before?

I laughed nervously. "Depression? Nah. Exhausted, maybe, but not depressed."

"It's nothing to be ashamed of. The hormone shifts along with the lack of sleep and anxieties around motherhood are bound to have an effect." She spoke in a soothing tone but it still felt like a criticism. A weakness. "You don't always have to be on the verge of a breakdown to be depressed."

"I know that," I scoffed, "but it's not as if I'm crying all the time." More than normal, admittedly, and living on my nerves was becoming the new normal for me. "It's sweet of you to worry about me, but there's really no need."

"When was the last time you got stuck into crafting? Really losing yourself in it?"

It was as though her eyes were drilling into me. It felt like a test.

"Crafting?" A laugh escaped my lips. "I've not got time for it these days. I'm a bit busy being a mum."

"And you're a great mum to Scarlett. You're patient and loving and so attentive. But that doesn't mean you need to lose your whole self. It's fine to hold a bit back, you know. A little corner of Sophie that's not Mummy."

She was trying to be nice, but my teeth were grinding defensively with every sentence she uttered.

"You don't get it. Being a mum isn't a part-time job." In my bid not to let the tears of frustration that were brewing flow I was making an effort to keep my voice cool and calm. "It's not a hobby. It's brutal. On call, twenty-four-seven. When would I get the time to craft? Or the energy? As soon as Scarlett nods off I'm ready to join her but I've got a wedding to plan and..."

Eve held up her hand, effectively cutting me off mid-flow.

"You've got to look after yourself, and if you won't do it then I will. I can't stand by and watch you fall apart like this. In all the time I've known you I've never seen you like this. You've lost your shine." A sad smile crept across my friend's face. "You look like the weight of the world is on your shoulders. Let me carry some of the load."

That was it, no way of keeping the tears at bay a moment longer. The floodgates opened.

"Hey." Eve threw her arms around me, squeezing me into a hug so tight I couldn't move. She was a human straitjacket. "You're okay, I've got you."

My shoulders juddered, but Eve's grip didn't loosen. If anything she held on tighter than before.

The sensation was overwhelming, my brain and body breaking down in unison. I'd been clinging on for such a long time but it was too much. I was unravelling in Eve's arms.

I couldn't tell you how long we stayed like that, Eve calming me with soft words and strokes of the hair. The tears flowed freely creating winding tracks down my cheeks until they reached my lips, the sting of salt sharp in my mouth.

"I didn't want to upset you. I just wanted you to know that I'm here for you. Always. It hurts me to see you struggling alone."

"But I'm not alone. There's Max and our families. Thousands of women do it without any help at all. And all those mums in the third world who don't have sterilisers and Infacol and all the other things I need to get through the day. How do they do it? Is it me? Maybe I wasn't cut out to be a mum after all."

"That's nonsense, you're one of the most maternal people I know. Think about Summer." It was impossible not to smile thinking about my ex Darius's daughter, precocious and precious and sharp as a whip. "She adores you and now Scarlett does too. If anyone was meant to be a mum it was you. Scarlett's one lucky little lady."

"But I'm tired all the time. Not just a bit, absolutely shattered to the core. I can't think straight. I went to the corner shop to get a pint of milk and didn't even look before crossing the road. A guy in a 4x4 almost hit the pram, he had to do an emergency stop. Then he wound the window down to tell me I should be more careful, but I'm functioning on autopilot. I didn't even see his bloody car coming."

No mention of his anger, nor what happened after. Being tired and emotional was one thing, wondering what it'd be like to jump into the Tyne was a whole different ball game. Eve would think I'd lost the plot. Hell, even I thought I'd lost the plot.

"I could have dropped you some milk. Don't feel you have to go out when you're not up to it."

I let out a sigh. "But then I'd never leave the house. You said yourself that I don't go out if I can help it and I thought I was doing a good job of hiding how much I'm struggling. What I need is more coffee. Or stronger coffee."

"What you need," Eve says firmly, "is to speak to a doctor. There's no shame in getting help when you need it."

"For being tired?"

"To talk about how you're feeling. That fatigue might be a sign of postnatal depression, and a GP or health visitor would be able to give you advice or even medication if you need it."

"I don't want medication. I've heard people on antidepressants talking about being dizzy and lethargic."

My friend smiled kindly. "Would that be any different to how you are now? And anyway, not everyone feels like that on antidepressants. I certainly don't."

I had to take a moment to pause, making sure my jaw hadn't actually dropped. Eve on antidepressants? She's always so practical, so together.

"You?"

"Yes, me." She fumbled in her handbag before pulling out a silver blister pack. "I've been taking them since mum got ill. I felt like you – so, so tired but I couldn't rest. However exhausted I was I couldn't sleep at night. Anxiety's a bitch."

"Too bloody right."

"What I'm trying to say is that you don't have to hit rock bottom before reaching out for help. Promise me you'll talk to a healthcare professional?"

"I promise I'll think about it," I replied.

It was the best I could do.

CHAPTER 24

The silence reverberated like an echo, but I stubbornly refused to be the one to break it.

My eyes hovered nervously around the surgery as the GP studied my medical history on his computer, every so often tapping on his keyboard or clicking his mouse. The environment was sterile and cold, which was hardly surprising. An examination bed shrouded in a thin layer of tissue paper. A box of latex gloves. A rack holding flyers about heart attacks, strokes, arthritis, chlamydia. Metal bins with foot pedal bars. And a brilliant white strip light that I feared would give me a migraine.

"So, tell me what brings you here today." The doctor wasn't one I'd seen before. He was younger, bear-like, with a friendly face and a grizzly auburn beard.

Scarlett weighed heavy in my arms, but not as heavy as the guilt. That was leaden.

I'm doing it for her, I reminded myself. So I can be the best mum I can possibly be.

"I think I'm suffering from postnatal depression."

Blurting out the words was a release. Dr Irvine nodded, encouraging me to continue. There was no judgement in his eyes, which helped. It meant I could be one hundred per cent honest, with both him and myself.

"I'm so tired all the time, half the time I don't remember what I'm doing. I'm making lists because otherwise I'm forgetting things and crossing days off the calendar because I can't remember what day it is, they all bleed into one. I cry at everything. Adverts on the telly, especially the ones for animal charities. I cried because we'd run out of Hobnobs the other day. And I'm scared." I pulled Scarlett closer to me, the warmth of her little body a comfort.

Dr Irvine nodded again. "What is it that scares you?"

"It might be easier to tell you things that don't scare me." I was only half joking. "I'm scared of something happening to Scarlett. I'm so tired I'm making bad decisions." I mentioned the incident with the 4x4 and the thoughts I'd had on the bridge. "I wasn't planning to actually jump," I clarify, "but I could see why someone else might. And I've never been like that before, even on my worst days. And I'm scared my partner's going to leave me."

My soul laid bare, to a complete stranger. Somehow it was easier to tell him my problems than it had been talking to Eve, when I'd only felt able to talk about motherhood. Dr Irvine didn't know me and he didn't know Max. It gave me carte blanche to be completely open and honest.

"I can see how distressing that would be," the doctor said, nodding once more. "And what would you like to do?"

My eyes widened. He was asking me what I wanted, rather than prescribing by rote. It was refreshing, not to mention empowering. It reminded me of when me and Iris had been putting together my birth plan. Admittedly, that hadn't turned out exactly as expected, but knowing I had autonomy over my own body was exactly what I'd needed then and what I needed now.

"What are the options?"

"There's the medical route, where we would start you on a mild antidepressant and see how you get on. Are you breastfeeding? There are some that we don't recommend using if you are, but there are plenty of other options."

"Breastfeeding's a sore point, but not a problem."

"Or, if you'd prefer, we offer courses. Mindfulness, cognitive behaviour therapy, that kind of thing. There are in-person meetings as well as online, although I have to be honest, there is a long waiting list at the moment. Or you can do a mixture of both: the medical and therapeutic routes."

The thought of having to wait after taking the step of asking for help didn't appeal. The wedding was looming large at the forefront of my mind – I needed stamina and focus to ensure me and Max ended up with a day to remember for all the right reasons rather than a disaster that'd be best forgotten.

"I'd like to try the tablets. The groups sound good but time isn't exactly plentiful right now," I said with a smile, looking down at my daughter.

"I bet. So, let me tell you a bit more about the medication I'd like to prescribe..."

By the time he'd reeled off warnings about possible side effects and that I'd likely feel worse before I felt better (worse? It was possible to feel worse?) doubts were setting in. Did this really warrant pumping myself full of drugs? But, despite everything, I knew it was the only option.

I left the surgery with a green prescription slip and a buzz of pride at my core. I'd been brave, tackling my problems head on. Scarlett stared up at me, eyes agog, from where she was laid in the pram. She'd seen me admitting my weaknesses, asking for help. It didn't matter that she was far too young to realise what a momentous step I'd taken, what a huge leap she'd witnessed. The swell in my chest was there regardless. I was her role model, and I'd demonstrated courage. Maybe I wasn't such a dreadful mother after all.

CHAPTER 25

The peace as Scarlett slept was idyllic and an opportunity to crack on with the wedding planning. The notebook I'd bought especially for the occasion ('Mr and Mrs' screaming out from the front of it as a reminder, just in case I'd forgotten) was page after illegible page of notes punctuated by clippings from magazines of ideas I'd liked. The trouble was, nothing was coherent. I liked patterns and florals, pastels and brights. I liked tulips and peonies, lavender and roses. Trying to put together a theme or scheme was nigh on impossible and I could hear Tawna's voice in my head talking about how important it was for everything to tie neatly together. Her own wedding had been a full-scale event.

Tawna's interest in flowers had come in useful, as she'd been able to tell me which were in season in October (and therefore which would be cheapest). Hector had also kindly told me to help myself to dahlias from his garden, but it was hard to rely on them as it was impossible to predict how successful they'd be.

Time was running out and my head was pounding with the stress.

"Where do I even begin?" I muttered to myself, spreading the cuttings across the table. The lists of all the things that needed doing was still long – finding someone to do the cake, wedding favours and transport at the top of the list. All things I'd laughed about when Tawna was getting herself in a state, but now I was in her position it was easy to see how wedding planning could quickly get out of hand.

Like so much else in life there was an element of keeping up with the Joneses and with social media that was only getting worse. Weddings were competitive, and even though I didn't want a flashy ceremony or a Cinderella carriage a la Katie Price, it was important that our guests had a good day. Weddings weren't just expensive for the couple getting married, by the time you factor in drinks, outfits, gifts, travel and hotel stays it was enough to bring you out in a cold sweat each time an invitation landed on the doormat. With that kind of outlay, the guests deserved to enjoy themselves too.

I was still poring over pictures when Max got home from work, moving them from the "yes" pile to the "maybe" pile and then back again.

"Honey, I'm home!" he quipped, poking his head around the door. "Good day?"

"Good day." I'd made the decision not to talk to him about the doctor's appointment and the antidepressants until teatime. He'd want to get showered and changed after his long day at the shop. "You?"

He came and sat next to me, loosening the Windsor knot of his tie. A suit wasn't his normal work attire but I knew the area supervisor was paying a visit to the shop. "It's been really good. Better than really good." Excitement laced his tone, the words spilling out. "The shop's being put forward as the best branch in the country. Can you believe it? Out of eighty shops and they think mine could be a contender." He shook his head in disbelief. "I can't take it in. I know it's only in-house, but it's amazing to even be considered."

"That's great news but you shouldn't look so surprised. The amount of work you put in is what makes the shop as successful as it is. Not to mention the rather handsome man behind the counter."

I was joking, but Max had quite the fan club. Not only was he a hit with the older ladies who fell for his charm, his good looks attracted a younger clientele. I knew this first-hand, having met him in the shop after spotting a jumpsuit in the window I couldn't resist. Sixteen months, a house move and a baby later, here we were, planning our wedding.

"I think it's more to do with a good location, to be honest. Regular footfall is what makes the difference, and changing up the window displays. If they stay the same for too long people become blind to them."

"The good-looking guy helps, trust me."

And boy, was he looking good. The worn-around-the-edges appearance from interrupted sleep made him look rugged rather than washed out, the glimmer of sweat an attractive sheen rather than a sticky mess. His fair hair was ruffled from a day of him running his hands through it, his shirt sleeves pushed up to reveal defined forearms. I was one lucky, lucky lady.

"And there's me thinking it's all to do with hard graft," he joked, before rolling his eyes, all the while a huge grin taking over his face. "I'm not here just to be ogled."

"You're not," I agreed, reaching out and placing my hand on his knee, "although you are looking mighty fine. That's brilliant news about the nomination, but if anyone deserves it it's you. You're working all the hours God sends right now."

"I know." He winced. "It's hard being away from you and

Scarlett so much, but it's you I'm doing it for. I want to make you proud."

"You don't need to make us proud, we already are."

He leant in and placed a kiss on my cheek. "Thank you. You bring out the best in me."

His words sent a rush from my heart right down to my tummy, a twist of love spinning in my stomach.

"It's a good job we're getting married then, isn't it?" I gestured to all the paraphernalia spread across the table. "I've been trying to move forward with the planning but the days are running away from me. It's weird, even when it feels like me and Scarlett have had a quiet day it doesn't seem possible to find the time, the feeding and changing cycle's relentless. I'm worried we won't get everything organised. Either that or I'll forget something big."

"As long as there's you and me, that's all I need."

"I think we can manage that."

However, regardless of what Max said, I knew there was an expectation. There always is with weddings.

Reheated curry and a microwave packet of rice dished up in front of us, I braced myself to tell Max about my doctor's appointment. An anxious lump lodged in my throat that I couldn't swallow no matter how hard I tried, the jalfrezi looking less appealing with each passing moment.

I knew I was being ridiculous for worrying about his reaction. Max loved me and he'd never been anything other than caring and supportive. That didn't stop me from overthinking it all though.

Right, I thought, it's now or never.

And although never was appealing, I knew the right thing to do was speak to Max about how I'd been feeling.

A sip of water to wet my lips. Another swallow to try to dislodge the knot in my windpipe. It was time to woman up and vocalise.

"I went to the doctor's today." My voice was small, nervous. "I've not been coping very well and thought they might be able to help me."

The shock was evident on Max's face, but I carried on, scared that if I stopped talking I might never finish what I wanted to say.

"Eve spoke to me about postnatal depression. That it isn't just about being tearful but about feeling out of your depth or that you've lost a part of yourself. And you know what? It rang true. I love Scarlett and I love being a mum but it's so much harder than I ever thought it'd be. So I've been given some tablets to help me cope."

I hadn't realised, but I'd been stirring my curry with my fork as I opened my heart to Max, ribbons of red sauce threaded through the yellow grains of rice.

"Why didn't you talk to me? I knew you were struggling but never thought it was this. I put it down to all the change over the last year."

"I wasn't being secretive, I promise. Until Eve mentioned postnatal depression I hadn't thought what I was going through was anything more than the effect of one too many sleepless nights. Now it makes sense, the doctor said it's quite common for women to feel like this after having a baby. Hormones, lack of sleep, the body recovering after pregnancy and birth – I suppose it's more of a surprise that not every new mum gets it."

"Mums certainly have a tougher job of it than the dads," Max agreed, through a mouthful of curry. "You've been amazing. Not that you weren't already amazing, but seeing you with Scarlett has shown how strong you are. It's made me love you more than I did before."

I let out a chuckle. Strong wasn't a word I'd have chosen to describe myself.

"What?" Max peered over his glasses, fork poised ready for another mouthful of food.

"Nothing."

"No, go on."

"I was just laughing at how you used the word strong when all day I'd been worrying about telling you because I was worried you'd think I was hopeless and weak."

Max's eyebrows arched in surprise. "You, hopeless? Never! Why would you think that?"

"Because I find life..." I paused, trying to find the word that best encompassed how I felt, "...challenging."

"That's because it is. In different ways for everyone."

"I've gone back to feeling the way I did when I first met you."

Max grinned. "Head over heels in lust?"

I poked out my tongue in retort. "Ha bloody ha," I said, although I was smiling right back at him. "I meant the inferiority complex. Thinking everyone's got a grip on life except me."

"They haven't, I promise you."

"Then how do they seem to be holding everything together so easily?"

"I can't answer that, I guess it'd be different for everyone. Lowering their expectations, maybe? Having a good support network?"

"But I'm out of my depth despite my support network being the best around."

"Nuh-huh." He shook his head. "I'm not having that. You might feel out of your depth, but I promise you're not. Anyone with eyes can see how you dote on Scarlett. She wants for nothing with you as her mam. And you made an appointment to get help when you needed it, that doesn't sound like the actions of someone out of their depth to me. If anything that's the sign of someone self-aware and in tune with their body."

The kind words had a positive effect, building up my battered self-confidence. I might not have dug deep enough to find the courage to tell Max about Gina and how bumping into her had been a factor in my decline, but I knew I would in my own good time. There's only so much bravery one girl can muster in a day and I'd reached my limit.

My appetite was slowly returning. Tentatively, I tasted a small forkful of the curry, spices bursting to life like a firework exploding in my mouth.

Everything was going to be okay.

I was going to be okay.

CHAPTER 26

Shopping for a dress wasn't the romantic experience I'd been led to believe it would be. All the films, all the TV shows – they lied. It was basically getting in and out of sample dresses made up of far more material than is humanly necessary. And did I mention the orange make-up stains from the foundation of people who'd tried the dress on before? It gave me the icks.

The shop assistant was friendly and down to earth, which was a far cry from the assistant who'd helped when we'd been hunting for Tawna's wedding dress. She patiently talked of sweetheart necklines and drop waists, explaining the cuts that would best flatter my shape.

First I tried on a lacy number, but knew it wasn't for me. Every lump and bump was accentuated and I felt as though I'd been wrapped up in one of the doilies Norma used to protect her sideboard.

Next was a full-blown princess dress; like Disney's version of Cinderella.

"Oh!" My mum raised her hand to her mouth. "You look so beautiful."

Tawna nodded her approval as I twisted my body to get a better view of myself in the mirror. "Yes, that's the one," she said. "Gorgeous. Max won't know what's hit him if you walk down the aisle in that."

Eve was quiet but I knew she was thinking the same as me. The dress was great, but it wasn't for me and definitely not for a woodland wedding in autumn. It'd be filthy by the time we were saying "I do" after trailing along the floor through the mud and leaves.

"I'm not convinced. It's very pretty, but I'd like to try something simpler, maybe tea length?"

The assistant nodded. "You've got great legs and I know just the dress. It's in the bridesmaid section, but no one would know if you didn't tell them."

She moved to the other side of the room, pushing swathes of pastel material aside and, like a magician pulling a rabbit out of a hat, returned with a dress that I knew was the one I was going to marry Max in. Even on the hanger I could tell the cut would suit me. As I had been blessed with an ample bosom a deep V always showed my assets in the best light, and Max was definitely a boob man.

An image of Gina flashed before me. She had curves too. Would she have chosen a dress like this if it had been her marrying Max? The very first time I met him, trying on a low-cut teal jumpsuit in the charity shop, he'd checked out my cleavage. To give him his dues it would have been hard to ignore my assets as I'd made sure they were front and centre. I didn't know where he'd met Gina. It might have been on a night out when she was wearing next to nothing – her figure was banging after having a baby so was probably even better before. Perky breasts. Tight skin over her stomach. The whole package.

I squashed down the negative thoughts as I tried on the dress, instead imagining how Max would respond to seeing me in it. The style suited me, I knew. Shoulder-skimming straps with a nipped-in waist; skirt falling to just below my knees as requested. The oyster satin changed colour in the light as I spun, always white, but with a hint of sky blue, pearlescent pink, mint green. Best of all, it had pockets.

The decision had already been made before I shared the look with my mum and bridesmaids. It was perfect. Practical and pretty. My thrifty side was also delighted – it was under budget. As the assistant said, no one would ever be able to tell it wasn't a wedding dress by design.

I stepped out of the changing room and into the shop.

Tears were welling up in Tawna's eyes, her lips pressed tightly together as she tried to stem the flow.

"How do I look?" I asked, already knowing the answer. My face was alight with happiness, I'd seen that in my reflection in the changing room mirror. And I was smiling. Everyone looks better when they're smiling. "Will I do?"

Eve nodded. "That's the one. You look really comfortable in it."

"I am. Plus..." I paused for dramatic effect, "...it has pockets!"

I pushed my hands into them to prove a point.

"I wouldn't have picked it out, but Eve's right. Not too flashy." Tawna gave me a thumbs up. "Perfect for our Soph."

My mum was at the end of the settee, close to a glass cabinet of satin shoes. She'd smiled when I first walked in but had quickly turned away. She wasn't even looking at me, instead her eyes firmly fixed on the footwear.

"Mum?"

In my head I had already bought the dress, but I couldn't get married in something my mum didn't like.

She turned to me. "You look so, so beautiful. You're going to be the most beautiful bride in the world." Our eyes connected and I knew she meant it. "These shoes match, see?"

I expected to see a pair of high heels which would probably be great with the dress in certain circumstances but not in a wood on an October day. Instead, on the bottom shelf, were a pair of ankle boots in the same fabric. I loved them immediately.

"Ooh, good eye," Tawna said approvingly.

"You don't think they'll get too muddy?"

Mum shook her head. "Even if they do you can change shoes before the reception. We can always buy a couple of pairs."

"Two pairs of shoes?" I laughed. "The same?"

"Why not?"

"It's a bit extravagant. Two pairs of shoes that I'll wear for a couple of hours each? I'd feel wasteful."

"I insist. I'll buy them for you. I'd already planned to pay for your dress. Me and your dad had agreed a limit but I had a little bit extra stashed away in case your taste was expensive. I know you like a designer frock."

Only a handful of the clothes in my wardrobe were labels since my destash, and those that were left had mainly been Vinted and Depop bargains. Mum wasn't to know that though. I'd downplayed the financial difficulty I'd found myself in. That was a) because I didn't want to worry my parents and b) because I'd convinced myself everyone else had their finances in order and to tell my mum and dad otherwise would prove how rubbish I was at adulting.

"I won't take no for an answer," she said, before turning to the assistant and saying, "Can we try the boots on the bottom shelf in a six please?"

I didn't dare argue.

Plus, I was grateful.

SEPTEMBER

CHAPTER 27

"Sorry!" Iris grimaced as she leant over the passenger seat to open the car door for me. "I know I'm stupidly late. Dina sicked up her breakie all over herself. The smell was vile, a wet wipe wasn't going to cut it. Jessie had to shower her down. I'll pay you back the money for this session seeing as we've missed half of it."

"Don't be ridiculous, these things happen. Babies aren't known for being predictable."

"Yeah, but if you'd have made your own way there you wouldn't have missed the session."

I buckled my seat belt and Iris looked over her shoulder as she pulled out into the road.

"To be honest I'm not sure I want to go anyway. I was only going because you were."

"I thought you enjoyed the baby massage classes?"

"I do, but..."

The words wouldn't come.

"But what? Spit it out."

"Georgina."

I looked to my right, trying to read Iris's expression. It gave me no clues.

"Georgina," she repeated thoughtfully. "The one who was late the first session? What's she done? Has she said something? Because if she's upset you then I'll show her no one messes with my friends."

I opened my mouth to respond but Iris was on a roll.

"Now you've said that it makes complete sense. She's got a negative vibe, it doesn't surprise me if she's rivalling *Mean Girls* for bitchiness."

Once more I tried to interject, but Iris didn't draw breath.

"Don't let one person put you off going. I know you've been feeling low lately," (I'd briefed her and my other Mummy friends on my trip to the GP via the group WhatsApp), "but she's not worth it. You and Scarlett are loving the classes, or at least, I thought you were. You have as much right to be there as she does so just stay out of her way and ignore any snidey comments."

I had to smile at her feistiness. It was one of the things I liked best about Iris, her no-nonsense approach to life. When I'd talked to her once about how I admired her tough exterior she'd laughed. "You have to have a thick skin when you're a family who doesn't meet what people think of as 'normal'. The amount of times I'm asked about my husband..." she shook her head. "You know the problem? This world's still too damn straight. Although I've got to admit I like playing with people. It's fun watching them squirm when I tell them about Jessie."

"I love how you're being so supportive, but Georgina's not done anything. Not to me, anyway."

Iris frowned. "All right, Cryptic Crystal. Spill."

My nostrils flared as I inhaled so deeply that a dizziness swirled in my skull.

"She's Max's ex-girlfriend. The one that got away," I added drily.

"You're kidding me." Iris took her eyes off the road momentarily and as she looked at me they were the size of two pence pieces. "Small world, huh?"

"That's one way of putting it."

I lurched forward, the seat belt digging into my neck as Iris slammed on the brakes as a car pulled out in front of her.

"Bloody idiot," she called out, honking her horn in anger. "Some people need to look where they're going."

"Hmmm." I rubbed my collarbone. "Some people do."

If she picked up on my sarcasm she ignored it. "So Georgina – miserable bitch-face Georgina – is Max's ex? Are you sure?"

"Of course I'm sure. His last girlfriend was called Gina, short for Georgina. She vanished without a trace and broke his heart."

"It's a common name, that doesn't mean she's his ex."

"I've seen a photo of them together, all cosied up, looking like love's young dream." The memory of finding the image with Andrea brought a horrible taste to my mouth. "It's her, no two ways about it. I don't want to see her."

"Yeah, I guess it's weird sitting opposite someone when you know they've seen your boyfriend's knob."

My lip curled up into a grimace. "Thanks for that. Really helpful."

She shrugged. "Just an observation."

There was a hush in the car, both babies peaceful in the back and me and Iris unsure where to take the conversation. The sensation of awkwardness prickled up my spine. Maybe I shouldn't have said anything after all.

"Look, if you really don't want to go, we don't have to. We're late anyway." She pulled off the A-road and into the retail park car park. "I think this requires some hard drinking." I must have looked puzzled as she smiled, adding, "Coffee, not alcohol. Unless you want alcohol, although no one's going to serve us at..." she paused, looking at the clock on the dashboard, "...quarter past nine."

"Wetherspoons would. Or The Eagle. I know the landlord. Not that I want alcohol."

"Large Americano, extra shot? I'll get takeout and bring them to the car. Don't want to disturb the sleepyheads."

"Thanks."

"Don't go anywhere," she said, rescuing her purse from the rainbow tote bag that had nestled in the passenger footwell near my feet.

"Where would I go?" I muttered to myself. I was hardly going to abandon Scarlett and Dana.

Iris returned shortly after armed with the much-needed coffee and two chocolate cookies. "I figured this was an emergency situation," she replied when I questioned her reasoning for returning with biscuits as well as coffee.

Over the next half hour I explained everything – Max's reluctance to commit to anyone following Gina ghosting him, how I'd stumbled across the photo of her in the Oakleys' family collection, the fear deep within me whenever I thought of telling Max that Gina and her child were in the same baby massage class as me and Scarlett.

"When was he with her? Is it possible he's Ronnie's dad?"

If I hadn't felt nauseous already, that pushed me over the edge. Even if it was an impossibility for Gina's son to be Max's it still made my stomach hurt.

"Not unless she had a two-year pregnancy."

"Well, that's something."

"But what should I do? Max doesn't even realise I know what she looks like. He wasn't there when I saw the photo, I was with his mum. The only other time I saw photos of Gina was when I was Facebook stalking."

"You've got to talk to him about it if it's bothering you."

"Easy enough to say but harder to do."

"Isn't everything?" Iris raised her eyebrows as she brought the paper cup to her lips. "But you can't let it fester."

"I know you're right, but..."

"No excuses. You spoke to him about your depression, you can talk to him about this too."

It was impossible to argue. She made it sound so simple.

The silence was broken by a small whinny which soon crescendoed into a full-blown cry of discontent. Dana was awake, which meant it was only a matter of time before Scarlett followed suit.

"I'll try," I said, as I unbuckled my seat belt and leant over into the back to put her dummy back in her mouth in a bid to keep her quiet for a little while longer. It was the best I could do.

The double shot of coffee combined with a burst of bravery, enabled me to face my demons (okay, maybe Gina wasn't a demon, but she certainly wasn't an angel either).

Max wasn't at work, having taken the day off to catch up with his friend, Iain, and although I didn't want to start an awkward discussion when he was going out with his mate, I knew my anxieties would return if I didn't spit it out.

"I've seen Gina." My voice was raised, because I couldn't run the risk of him not hearing me first time. I didn't think I'd have the guts to repeat myself.

His head jolted upright, jaw slack and grey-blue eyes sparkling. His reaction brought with it another wave of nausea, but there was no going back.

"She goes to the baby massage group I take Scarlett to," I started, looking away. I didn't want to see his face – it would only make me overanalyse. Instead, I carried on, "I didn't realise it was her at first, but then I saw a photo of her at your mum and dad's..."

He frowned. "What photo?"

"I don't know, from some wedding or other." I flipped my hand dismissively. "That's not what's important. She's still in Newcastle. I thought you should know."

Max blinked, then pushed his glasses up his nose. He didn't say a word.

The churning in my stomach increased, like a tumble drier on full-spin mode. It was painful, the lack of response. The ticking of the clock on the mantelpiece seemed louder than ever, the motor of our next-door neighbour's lawnmower might as well have been a pneumatic drill. Everything was at full volume.

I looked up, scared of what I might see. I knew Max loved me, I didn't doubt that, but there was still the fear that he might be thinking about the life he could have had with Gina, if things had turned out differently. Everyone has "what ifs", don't they?

"It doesn't surprise me that she's in Newcastle. I always suspected she'd got back together with the guy she was with before me and he lived in Byker."

I nodded slowly, still trying to interpret Max's body language, his expression, his tone... There was no sign of the disappointment I'd expected. He did look gobsmacked, granted, but I wasn't sure if that was down to me knowing what Gina looked like rather than her living in the area.

"You're not... upset?"

"About what? Sure, it hurt when she disappeared off the face of the earth. Doesn't do much for your ego when the person you thought you might have a future with ghosts you. But that was a long time ago."

"I didn't know how you were going to react." I took a deep

breath as I processed Max's reaction. "When you told me about her I thought she was the love of your life."

He reached out to my face, stroking his fingertips down my cheek. "The love of my life is right here with me."

"But she broke your heart! You told me!"

"She did. At the time I was a mess and it took me a long time to trust again." He paused, a slightly dopey smile appearing on his face. "Then I met you."

A rush of blood caused my cheeks to flush with love. "I was so scared."

"Scared? What of?"

"Scared that knowing she was around would make you think twice about being with me."

Somehow saying it out loud sounded ridiculous after Max's declaration, but the tears still came, relief.

"You and Scarlett are my whole world." He looked deep into my eyes and when I automatically looked down to try to hide the shame I felt for ever having doubted the level of his love for me, he placed his thumb under my chin, gently lifting my head until our eyes were level again.

"What I had with Gina never came close. Nothing would make me think twice about being with you. Every day I thank my lucky stars that you walked into the shop. You, Sophie Eliza Drew, are the best thing that has ever happened to me."

With that he pulled me into an embrace, my face smooshed against the soft brushed cotton of his T-shirt. We stayed like that for a very long time, a very long time indeed.

CHAPTER 28

Honesty was becoming easier. The more open I was about the things that were causing me distress, the more I was able to cope. There was still the initial panic whenever I told someone about my anxieties, especially when they were things I knew were minuscule issues that I'd built up to being ginormous in my head. Overall though, there had been a mental shift for the better.

That was how, on the day we were due to pay the balance for the reception venue, I told Max I wanted to bin the wedding plans which had taken up so much of my time and energy over the months.

His face fell until I shared the alternative that had been brewing away in the back of my mind.

"You said yourself that there's no need for all the fuss. Me, you and Scarlett, everything else is just for show. What's the point in bunting and canapés and Bucks Fizz? If both of us feel the same, that we just want to be married, it makes sense to elope. Then we get the day that we want without worrying about keeping everyone else happy."

"My parents might kill us for getting married without them there. And your parents. They're so excited for us."

"And they'll be excited when we tell them we got married."

Max scrunched up his nose. It looked unbearably cute. "Doubtful."

"They'll get over it." I was channelling Iris. "We can still have a party but the wedding itself doesn't need to be an overpriced circus."

I felt lighter, as though a tonne-weight had been lifted from my shoulders.

"And you're sure about this? I don't want you to look back at our wedding photos in years to come and regret not having all the bells and whistles."

"One hundred per cent sure. None of that matters, all that matters is us."

"We'd better look into how we go about planning an elopement then." He grinned.

I didn't need telling twice, immediately setting about pulling up information on my phone. Getting married in Newcastle was an option, of course. The register office was based in the middle of town and we were familiar with it after being there so recently to make Scarlett official. There was always the risk people would find out about the wedding though, with the banns being posted prior to the ceremony, which was why it made perfect sense to me that we should run away to Gretna Green.

When I shared the idea with Max, he loved it. I should have known he would, being a romantic softie at heart. Within the hour it was booked and I began contacting people to cancel our big, fat, Newcastle wedding.

"This feels right, doesn't it?" I said, scoring a line through the details of the florist I'd provisionally booked.

Max nodded. "Definitely."

"I can't wait to marry you, Maxwell Oakley."

"And I can't wait to marry you, Sophie Drew."

The hardest part of planning a secret wedding was, unsurprisingly, keeping it secret. My tactic of just not mentioning our upcoming nuptials would have worked had it not been for the fact everyone was expecting an autumn wedding.

I didn't want to lie to our friends and family so became adept at changing the subject whenever anyone mentioned how they'd heard news that late October was going to be scorching. Tawna, being a wedding obsessive, was sending daily texts asking how she could help as the big day got closer, and guilt did assuage me every time I sent a sunny, "all in hand, but thanks!" as a reply.

My mum's reaction to us having a night away so close to the wedding made me suspect she knew something was going on.

"And I thought the honeymoon was supposed to happen after the wedding," she joked.

Using my mental health as a reason for taking a much-needed break felt wrong, even if technically it was true, but for the glaring omission of the major life event that would be happening on our night away.

"I don't know if I'll be able to keep it quiet until the day," I whispered to Max. "Look at my forehead, I'm dripping!"

I wiped the back of my hand across my hairline, grimacing at the sweat brought on by nerves.

"Only two weeks to go now." He leant in, his lips so close to my earlobe that they caught it as he spoke. "And then we'll be husband and wife."

The thought made me fizz from head to toe.

"Two weeks of keeping this to ourselves though," I

murmured, wondering if there were any other tactics I could use to dodge the barrage of questions our loved ones asked every day. "Can we go into hiding?"

Max laughed. "A bit radical."

"But necessary. It's impossible to avoid everyone's questions. I know they're asking because they care, but still..."

"Fourteen days. Then we can shout it from the rooftops."

I couldn't wait.

&

Two nights. That's how long we were going to be in Scotland for, but Max's Mini was still bursting at the seams. Most of it was Scarlett's – pram, travel cot, all the day-to-day necessities that took up more space than you expected. Then there was Max's suit bag, holding the slate-grey suit he always wore for special occasions hanging in the back, with my dress boxed up. Thank heavens I'd not gone for a full-skirted affair, because there wasn't room for the dress I'd chosen let alone a meringue.

"Now, are you sure we've got everything we need?" Max slammed the boot closed, leaning against it to ensure the lock had caught securely. He grinned mischievously. "Because I'm not sure you remembered the kitchen sink."

"Very funny," I replied, with a droll roll of my eyes. "This is the bare minimum. Most of it's Scarlett's."

"That's it, blame our four-month-old daughter." He laughed, and I playfully swiped at his arm.

"It is! What's that Shakespeare quote about being little? I think it should be adapted for the modern era – 'though she be little, she be in need of lots of very large equipment'."

"Old Willy will be turning in his grave." Max walked around to the door on the driver's side, climbing in as I strapped Scarlett into her seat before joining Max in the front. "Are you ready? Sure there's nothing else we need?"

"I'm sure." I couldn't keep the smile from my face as he turned the key in the ignition, the engine roaring into life. "Let's get married!"

The converted barn which was to be our home for the next two nights was every bit as lovely as the Airbnb description had suggested. Spacious, with a whitewashed walls and exposed brickwork combination that was bang on trend, a gorgeous decked area overlooking a well-kept garden bursting with blousy dahlias in every colour of the rainbow. The bedroom was on a mezzanine level, a metal four-poster bed keeping with the industrialist décor but softened by milky-white teddy bear throws and cushions.

"You did well finding this place." Max flopped back onto the bed, still wearing his Adidas trainers. "It's as nice as the hotel you tried first."

"Feet!" I exclaimed, and he quickly slung his legs so the striped shoes dangled over the edge of the mattress. "And I am pretty proud of myself. It would've been nice to stay at Smiths but we had left it late. We'll be all right here, won't we?" I said to Scarlett, jiggling her on my hip before sinking down onto the bed to join my husband-to-be.

An hour later, after a much-needed power nap for all three of us, we freshened up before heading to the Blacksmiths Shop at Gretna Green. Our wedding ceremony was the best part of twenty-four hours away but we were still curious to see the place in person to check it was as quaint as the images we'd seen online.

We needn't have worried. It was exactly as the pictures had shown; bursting with olde-worlde charm. If anything, it was prettier than I'd expected.

A couple of newlyweds held hands as they posed for photos, two brides in sleek ivory silk dresses. Their joy was infectious, the taller of the two smiling so widely that her face was ninety per cent gums.

"Look at the brides," I said to Scarlett, who was more interested in a one-legged pigeon perched on a nearby wall. "Don't they look pretty?"

Seeing them together, radiating happiness, made me think of Iris and Jessie. It was hard to believe that as recently as 2014 same-sex couples couldn't get married in England, Scotland or Wales. The devotion etched on the faces of the women in front of us, along with the commitment in my friends' relationship, was undeniable. It made it even harder to understand why it had taken so long for these supposedly forward-thinking, liberal countries to allow men to marry men and women to marry women.

"That'll be us tomorrow." Max wrapped his arm around my shoulder as the photographer instructed the couple to kiss. "Let's hope we'll be as happy as those two lovebirds."

"We will be."

"You sound very sure of yourself."

"And why shouldn't I be? You and me against the world, now and forever."

He squeezed my shoulder. "And I'd put money on us being the victors."

CHAPTER 29

"Wakey wakey, sleepyhead," I sang, placing the strong cup of coffee on the bedside table. "We've got a big day ahead of us."

Max rolled over, burying himself under the duvet. "Too tired." The words were muffled by the bedding. "Ten more minutes."

"Nuh-huh. No chance. You need to look after Scarlett while I go and shower. No one wants a smelly bride."

Whether it was the b-word or my tone of voice that spurred him into action I don't know. Either way, Max groaned as he plumped up the pillows behind him, before welcoming our daughter into his outstretched arms.

"You don't look like you had much sleep. It was me who was up half the night with this one."

"I know, and I'm grateful. Sorry I tossed and turned all night."

"You're not getting cold feet, are you?" I asked, as I rifled through the suitcase to find the strapless bra and seamless pants I'd bought especially to wear under my wedding dress. "No second thoughts?"

"None whatsoever. I can't believe you even need to ask."

"Just checking," I said with a contented smile.

"I swear I had about an hour's sleep. My brain wouldn't switch off. I kept worrying about whether the rings were safe and if I'd remembered to pack my tie."

"Welcome to my world," I joked, as I found the paper bag containing my underwear, "where overthinking is a normal part of every single day."

"You're amazing, you know that." I could see him squinting at me, his short-sightedness making him strain to focus. "You're amazing, and I love you."

"I love you too," I said, smiling to myself as I closed the bathroom door behind me.

The shower was invigorating. If I hadn't got a wedding to go to, I'd have happily stayed under the spray until my skin wrinkled like a raisin, but we were expected at the world-famous Blacksmiths Shop at noon.

Max's voice floated from the bedroom as I moisturised, my heart full at the sound of him chattering away to Scarlett.

I wriggled into my new underwear, so much more rigid than the sets I wore and washed to oblivion, and turned to study myself in the mirror. The reflection looking back at me looked older than I was in my mind's eye and at first glance I saw my mum rather than myself. But it was the mum of my childhood, not the woman she was now – still well presented, as was expected in her job as a beauty rep, but with creases of experience lining her face. Not only did I look like my mum had in photos thirty years ago, my body was unfamiliar to me.

Since having Scarlett I'd not really looked at my shape – I'd tried not to, for fear of what I might see. My figure had always erred towards the voluptuous and the curves were all still there, the wobbly bits wibbling a bit more, but still an hourglass shape which Max had always said he loved. And my boobs, I knew he liked those. Which was just as well, because they were hard to miss, especially with the super-scaffolding bra ensuring they stayed where they were meant to.

"Not bad, Soph," I said, remembering Eve's words about speaking to myself as she would speak to me. "Not bad at all."

I slipped my arms into the towelling bathrobe before tying it closed, then wrapped a towel around my dripping wet hair.

Before heading back to my family, I gave the woman in the mirror one last look.

Sophie Drew smiled back at me, a woman who was loved by her friends, her family and her fiancé, but most importantly, by herself.

CHAPTER 30

"Wow." Max's eyes worked their way slowly down my body, taking in every inch. "Just... wow."

I gave a little shimmy, swishing the multiple layers of fabric like a flamenco dancer. My choice of wedding dress wasn't flouncy, but the skirt was gorgeously swishy, mimicking my movements as it swayed along with me, the light casting pastel rainbow shades on the fabric.

"Scrub up okay, don't I?" I couldn't stop a gormless grin from spreading across my face. For the first time in a long time I felt happy in my own skin.

"Wow," he said once more, blinking from behind his glasses. "What did I ever do to deserve you? You always look gorgeous, but..." He paused, shaking his head and I anticipated another "wow" that didn't come.

"The dress helps."

Max shook his head. "It's gorgeous, but not as gorgeous as the woman wearing it."

I couldn't resist giving another twirl, memories of pulling off very similar moves on the dance floor at a holiday camp twenty years prior making my already huge grin spread further still.

The skirt flared out, a perfect circle of silk blurring as I spun. It felt exactly as it had when I was spinning on the shiny yet sticky floors in the bar at the resort, as though I was dizzy; the twirling and twisting along with pure happiness giving an adrenalin rush that could rival any chemical high.

When I stopped, the light-headed sensation swirling around my brain, a giggle formed in my chest.

It was my wedding day, mine and Max's.

The sun was shining, the birds were singing and my heart was overflowing with love for my little family.

"What's so funny?" Max asked, sliding both hands around my waist.

"Nothing," I replied through my laughter. "I'm just happy. Deliriously happy."

From her buggy, Scarlett chuckled. Baby laughter really is the most infectious thing and before long the three of us were laughing so hard we were close to tears.

Max pulled back the cuff of his shirt, looked at his watch and then bit down on his lip. "We'd better head off. Our slot's in half an hour."

"Let's do this. Let's go and get married!"

The sky overhead as we strolled to the Blacksmiths was the purest, blemish-free blue; the large sculpture of two clasped hands bathed in sunshine, the weather more suited to July than late September. That said, the gentle breeze was welcome, especially as my heart was racing with excitement. The secrecy of the day made it feel vaguely naughty, as though we were waiting to be caught out and told off. Other happy couples were milling around, some with wedding guests but many, like us, holding the life-changing ceremony without. It gave the whole place an aura of utter joy and celebration, as infectious as Scarlett's giggles had been back at the cottage.

On our way to the venue we passed a stone sculpture of a couple embracing, the open space outside the Blacksmiths flanked with flower beds of reds, whites and pinks which matched the overflowing hanging baskets decorating the whitewashed walls of the building.

Romance was everywhere; in the padlocks couples placed to commemorate their union and the unique bass-like tone of bagpipes filling the air, the players in tartan dress. Horseshoes destined to bring good luck festooned the archway where a bride and groom posed for photographs.

There was a comfort in the sense of tradition and the knowledge so many couples had taken the very same steps as us as they entered their own marriages. I'd read about the history of Gretna Green. For over two hundred and fifty years young lovebirds had flocked to the village to tie the knot, originally being blessed by the blacksmith who'd strike the anvil to announce each marriage. That ritual remained, although the blacksmith had long been replaced by a registered celebrant.

I paused as we stepped into the building, taking a mental snapshot to hold on to for all of time. The love of all the couples who'd gone before was palpable and as we were welcomed and ushered towards the anvil room where the ceremony would take place, I reached out to take Max's hand in mine. We were really going to do it, we were getting married!

The room looked just how it had on the photos I'd seen online – exposed wooden struts supported the roof and examples of the metalwork that would have originally been forged in the space lined the back walls where the white paint peeled off the stonework. The anvil was the centrepiece, placed on a wooden plinth on the slabbed floor.

The ceremony itself was a blur of love with Max and I totally fixed on each other as we made our vows. Scarlett, on her best behaviour, was in my arms throughout, even during the exchanging of rings. It was a juggling act, but a nice one. As the celebrant announced Max and I were husband and wife, his hammer clanging against the anvil to seal our vows, our daughter gave a gurgle of delight.

"Happy?" Max asked, as he leaned in for our first married kiss.

"Happy," I confirmed, the warm fizz of contentment bubbling in my chest.

I hadn't expected to feel different, but I did. As Max took my hand in his, steering Scarlett in the buggy with the other, I savoured the moment. The cool band of metal on the third finger of his left hand was unfamiliar but so, so right. A sign of our love and commitment, a symbol that told the world we were together – a team.

We'd opted for the simple ceremony without any extras, so instead of formal photographs taken by an official photographer we accosted another couple to take a handful of snaps on Max's phone. The shots weren't the clearest, but the smiles on our faces meant there was no doubt about our happiness. Even Scarlett looked at the camera, eyes startled by the unnecessary flash, lips parted in a gasp. I loved the photos. I loved the memories. But most of all I loved Max and Scarlett – my husband and my daughter.

CHAPTER 31

Waiting for my parents to answer the door was like waiting to be told off as a child. Nerves jangled, my stomach knotted. No one would have believed we were about to share the happy news of our nuptials because I was an emotional wreck, picking at the loose skin around my nails. I knew it was a bad idea, the manicure I'd treated myself to was still looking good, but wouldn't be when the skin around each nail was a red flaky mess.

"Stop panicking," Max whispered, "they'll be happy for us."

"Happy for us but gutted we didn't invite them," I corrected, as the blur of my mum's silhouette appeared behind the door's frosted glass panelling.

There was time for one final deep breath before the door opened, my mum's perfectly made-up face beaming at us.

"What a lovely surprise! We weren't expecting you today." I could see the cogs in her brain turning as a frown appeared on her face. "It's a Wednesday. What are you doing off work, Max? Holiday day?"

He looked at me encouragingly.

"We had a night away in Scotland," I reminded her, wishing

Dad was also in the hallway so I wouldn't have to say it twice. Once was bad enough, the disappointment was going to be terrific. "A last-minute thing."

I waved my hand dismissively, as though by downplaying it I would somehow lessen her upset.

"Sophie." Her hand reached out and clutched at my fingers, the way it must have so many times when I was a child. She held it up, taking in the white gold band on the third finger of my left hand, and I knew the secret was out. "What's this?"

She gawped at me. Scarlett's cry was a welcome distraction. I loosened my hand and took her from Max, holding her close to my chest and rocking from side to side.

"You know how I've been anxious lately?"

My mum nodded a wordless reply.

"Planning a big wedding was making me worse. Making my mental health worse. With no sleep and then Scarlett's colic and teething... I couldn't cope. So we went to Gretna Green and got married the day before yesterday."

"But it's only a month until the wedding."

"A month is a long time when you feel like you can't even get through an hour." I shifted from foot to foot, shushing Scarlett. "We would have loved you to be there with us, but if we invited you and Dad we'd have had to invite Andrea and Hector, and then all our siblings. There's no such thing as a small wedding in a big family."

Mum's expression changed from confusion to disappointment, crumpling like a shirt that's been put through the tumble dryer. "But your dress... it was so beautiful and now you won't get to wear it."

"I still wore the dress, Mum. And we'll have a party on our original date and get dressed up again so you can still wear your outfit."

"And what about Summer? She was expecting to be your bridesmaid. The poor girl will be heartbroken."

Max stood there silent, but the palm of his hand against the flat of my back gave me a strength I didn't know I had within me.

"Summer will be fine. She can wear her dress and have her hair done for the party and it's not like she hasn't been a bridesmaid before and I've robbed her of her only chance. And before you say it, I know Tawna will be devastated, loving weddings as much as she does, but she'll get over it. It was *our* wedding," I said, looking to my husband for support, "not anyone else's."

"We never planned to upset anyone, Mrs Drew," Max said, reverting to formality rather than first-name terms, as he always did when wanting to ensure he was being super polite. "You know how much I love Sophie, and I'd do anything in my power to look after her as best as I can. She was wearing herself out trying to plan a big wedding and it wasn't doing her health any good, mental or physical. Can we come in and have a talk about it over a cup of tea and a slice of your chocolate cake? I'm sure you've got some stashed away in a tin waiting for a special occasion."

"And we can show you the photos," I added, knowing my mum wouldn't be able to resist. "It was such a beautiful place, Mum. So romantic. And we stayed in a converted barn with a four-poster bed!"

I could see her softening. Max's charm and my bribery working a treat.

"Come on," she said, stepping to one side and creating a pathway for us. "And we'd better get your dad in. He's pottering about in the garden, weatherproofing the fence for winter. He'll be ready for a cuppa by now."

"Oh, Sophie." Dad let out a sigh. "You look beautiful. Radiant."

We'd printed out the pictures in anticipation, knowing Mum and Dad would appreciate having their own hard copies. One had already taken pride of place on top of the mantelpiece, waiting for a frame to match the photos of my siblings, Nick and Anna, on their wedding days.

"I felt it too. It's been a long time since I felt so good about myself. It helped having Max being so complimentary."

"You make it sound like I'm not normally," Max said with a laugh.

"You know what I mean, it gave me a real boost. I felt like a princess for a day."

"And you looked like one," Mum said fondly, tracing her finger along the picture. "My beautiful, beautiful girl. And Scarlett and Max look lovely."

"It's the smiles," Dad chipped in. "All three of them look so happy."

"I know you would have loved to be there, but we hope you understand why we did it this way." I smiled apologetically. "Sorry you didn't get to walk me down the aisle, Dad. I know you were looking forward to it."

"Walking you down the aisle would have been a pleasure, but what gives me the most happiness is seeing you happy. The day I married your mother was one of the best of my whole life and even now I think back to it and can remember every little detail."

"He does, you know," Mum said knowingly. "Someone walked past wearing Anais Anais and he said it smelt like me. That's the perfume I used to wear in those days, before I started working for Avon."

"I hope I'll remember everything too." Max smiled. "Although Scarlett's explosive nappy can fade from the memory."

"It was all up his sleeve," I shared, the pungent stench and gooey mustard poop still very clear in my mind. "I was just glad it wasn't me carrying her."

I was only half joking.

We laughed more as we pored over the photos, talking about the wedding, Gretna and the forthcoming party.

"It'll be as much of a celebration as we'd planned before, but will just be an evening do. Pie and peas are still on the menu."

"With gravy? You can't have pie and peas without gravy."

"There will be gravy," I confirmed. "You won't miss out, Dad."

As we prepared to leave, gathering up the array of muslin squares and shoving them into the changing bag, Max offered one last apology. "I'm genuinely sorry you weren't able to be there with us yesterday."

My mum drew him in for a hug, and although her voice was quiet I could hear her words. "Thank you," she said. "For making my little girl smile again."

Luckily, Max's parents were equally as understanding (at least, to our face. Only the miserable cat, Bunty, looked disgusted with us, but she looks like that most of the time with her hoity-toity nose-in-the-air demeanour, so I didn't take offence).

"We'll have to party extra hard at the reception instead." Hector moved his hands above his head in a motion that looked suspiciously like the "big fish, little fish, cardboard box" move. "Andrea, can you rig up the Christmas lights to my chair that day? You can call it an art installation."

"Oh, behave." She laughed, her voice full of affection.

"She thinks I'm joking," Hector flicked his head in his wife's direction, "I'm deadly serious. The party doesn't start till I roll in."

"You've never seen my dad in action, have you?" Max shook his head in mock exasperation. "I've got terrible memories of him teaching everyone the moves to Agadoo at my sixth birthday party. We don't want a repeat performance."

Hector wagged his index finger at his son. "You loved every minute of it. That and the one where everyone sits on the floor and pretend they're rowing a boat. What's it called, Andrea?"

"'Oops Upside Your Head'."

"That's the one. In fact, you loved any song with a dance."

"I never knew that."

Suddenly I felt bad about denying him a first dance. It felt like one moment in the spotlight too far and as most of my time dancing was back in my clubbing days I'd feel naked without glow sticks to hide behind.

"He was always the first up on the dance floor at school discos too," Andrea reminisced. "And he won a competition at a holiday camp. I think that was for dancing to 'Saturday Night'."

"I did love Whigfield," Max admitted, turning to me and adding, "I think it was that video of her with the hairdryer. There weren't any girls as sexy as that at my primary school."

"I'd hope not! You were only about seven!" Andrea rolled her eyes. "I don't know, it's a good job you've already put a ring on Sophie's finger or she might be changing her mind finding out all about your past."

"I love hearing about it. There's lots I wish I knew about him. Sometimes I wish we'd gone to the same school."

Max's eyes widened, his lips scrunching up. "You'd have thought I was an idiot. Anything for a cheap laugh. The amount of times my report said I was class clown..." His voice trailed off, a dopey grin taking over his face as he reminisced.

"You weren't so bad." Andrea took a sip of her elderflower

cordial. "Dale was the one who messed about the most. Still does! Sometimes I doubt he'll ever leave home."

"We thought the same about Max when he moved back though," Hector reminded her. "We joked about how we'd never be the empty nesters all our friends were. And we were probably right."

Max tutted. "And there was I thinking I was doing everyone a favour by moving back home when you were struggling."

"You were brilliant," his dad reassured him. "You really helped your mum when I was at my worst. I know it wasn't easy pushing me around in this old thing." He tapped the side of his wheels. "It's a lead weight."

Andrea laughed, then pulled a face. "The wheelchair's not the only thing that's a lead weight, all that cake's gone straight to your tummy."

"Middle-age spread." Hector patted at the spare tyre around his waist. "Inevitable, especially when I can't walk as much as I'd like."

His wife affectionately massaged his shoulder, the bond between them clear even after all the years and what had been thrown at them. It made me excited for what my own marriage would hold.

"I think we're past middle-age, love." Andrea bent down, planting a kiss on her husband's forehead. "Can we say we're in the prime of our lives?"

Hector nodded. "I'd go along with that. Our children are all grown up, grandchildren bring sunshine into our lives and we're making time for what's important. Which reminds me, with all the excitement about the wedding you haven't told Max and Sophie about your latest project."

All eyes focused on Andrea, other than Scarlett's (but, to be fair, she was out for the count).

"Come on, don't keep us waiting," Max egged on. "Sounds exciting."

"It is, rather." Andrea beamed, her eyes sparking bright with excitement. "The community centre was looking for an artist to create a mural in their main hall. Images of Newcastle, that kind of thing. I submitted a design months back, not expecting it to come to anything, but yesterday I had a phone call asking if I was interested in the project." Pride radiated from her as she continued. "Naturally, I said yes. My first real job as an artist! And I'm getting paid. I'd have happily done it for free."

"That's fantastic, they must know talent when they see it." Max hugged his mum in a warm embrace of congratulation.

"That's brilliant." I was genuinely thrilled for my mum-in-law. She'd put her dreams on hold for so long to raise her boys but now it was time for her to reach out with both hands and grab every opportunity. "We'll have to come to the grand unveiling."

A becoming flush of cerise spread over Andrea's cheeks at being the centre of attention. "Oh, that's a while away yet. Lots of hours to put in before then."

"Her design is very intricate," Hector added. "It's got everything from the bridge to brown ale to Alan Shearer celebrating. It couldn't be more representative of Newcastle if it tried. She thought of everything."

"I approve of the Magpies being included. My dad will too, although he'd probably argue Keegan should be on there somewhere."

"I did think about it, but in the end opted for Cheryl."

Max's head turned as he did a double take. "Cheryl Cole? Or whatever name she goes by these days? What's she done to deserve being on it?"

"Girls Aloud were very successful back in the day," I said, as

Andrea gave me a conspiratorial wink. "Sold out arena tours, number one hits, the lot," I added, struggling to stifle my giggles.

"There's that one song of theirs that always gets me up and dancing," Andrea continued, doing the "step to the left, click fingers, step to the right, click fingers" dance that was so popular with mums. She started to hum, but none of us were any the wiser about which song it was that had got her moving. "What's it called?" She closed her eyes as though that'd help her bring it to mind. "Got it!" she said eventually, "'Sex Machine'."

"That's James Brown, love," Hector corrected.

Max started singing the soul hit, until Andrea shushed him. "Not that one, I know that one's James Brown. A different Sex Machine song."

She proceeded to sing the track and it wasn't long until we realised what she was getting at.

"You mean 'Love Machine', not 'Sex Machine'." I laughed.

"Not that it matters, seeing as Cheryl Cole isn't on my mural. She did come up on a list of famous Geordies though, just above Jimmy Nail."

"Please tell me he's not on the mural either."

Andrea shook her head. "The woman running the centre specifically asked for Ant and Dec. I think she had a crush on one of them, not that I can tell them apart."

Hector rolled his eyes. "They look nothing alike! And they make it easy by always standing in the same places, Ant on the left and Dec on the right."

"Which is fine when they're together but not much good when they're apart." Andrea rolled her own eyes back at him, in an even more exaggerated fashion. "One of them got married recently and the pictures were all over the papers. I still didn't know which one of them it was." She shrugged.

"It said 'Ant's Big Day' right above the photo," her husband laughed, "and she was still none the wiser."

"I was tired," she replied defensively, but she was laughing along too.

This was what I loved about the Oakleys, the light-heartedness, the gentle ribbing of each other which never veered over into anything malicious. It felt good to be a part of it, truly a family member.

CHAPTER 32

Tawna cried real tears when I told her about the wedding. I'd expected a negative reaction, but not one as intense as hers.

"I can't believe you'd get married without us there," she said with a sniff, gesturing her hand between herself and Eve. "I would never have done that. Wouldn't even have considered it."

"We're different types of people," I pointed out, although I was blatantly stating the obvious. From our looks to our demeanours, me and Tawna were close to polar opposites. "You know it wasn't personal. The big wedding was perfect for you and Johnny, but not for us. It was making me stressed worrying about wedding breakfasts and photographers and everything else."

"It's supposed to make you stressed." She gave me a "duh" look. "That's part of the fun of planning a wedding."

I bit my tongue rather than mentioning how being in Tawna's company when she was planning her wedding was anything but fun. The term Bridezilla could have been coined for her.

"I have postnatal depression," I said calmly. "I'm on tablets to help me cope. It wasn't top of my agenda to have the wedding day to end all wedding days." That wasn't meant as a bitchy dig, but as Tawna's face fell I wondered if I'd been too harsh. "Being married was what mattered to me and Max, and as much as we'd have loved everyone there it wasn't the most important factor."

Tawna opened her mouth to speak but Eve interjected, her usual damage limitation strategy coming into play whenever me and Tawna came to blows.

"We understand, don't we?" She fixed a stare, eyebrows jumping towards her hairline, prompting Tawna to back her up. "And we're thrilled for you. Since Max has been in your life you've been happier than you've been in a long time."

"Of course we are. But I'd have loved to have been with you on your wedding day. Having you and Eve with me on my own wedding day kept me sane."

"And, I'm saying this with complete and utter love," I said, reaching out and taking her hands in mine, "not having guests at mine is what kept me sane."

Eve's sharp inhalation of breath made me wonder if I should have been more careful with my words, but it was the truth. Looking after myself had to be the priority.

"I promise the party is going to be as much a celebration as it was always going to be. You'll still have chance to get your hair and nails done and wear your dresses."

"But we weren't there to help you get ready for the actual wedding, nor to see Max's face when he first clapped eyes on you in your dress. We didn't even get to have a hen do."

Genuine sorrow was in both her words and expression. Yes, Tawna could be self-centred and materialistic but her fierce loyalty to her friends and family was unrivalled.

"You will be by my side through the marriage though, and I'm sure there'll be times when I need you to rant at or cry on. We've always been there for each other before so there's no reason for that to change now."

"Speaking of which," Eve interjected again, "Tawna, you need to tell Sophie about the anniversary present Johnny gave you."

My gaze automatically scanned my friend's hands for a new ring – Johnny knew Tawna was old school and an eternity ring would be an ideal gift to celebrate a year of marriage – but there were no new rings, only her usual wedding band and the enormous diamond engagement ring. No necklace either, and she wasn't a big wearer of earrings. I started to think of alternatives – matching tattoos weren't their style, and designer heels, which were very much Tawna's style, didn't seem special enough seeing as my friend had a habit of buying a new pair every couple of weeks.

I wasn't prepared for what she said.

"He's bought me a farm." She gave an excited squeal as I looked at her, bemused.

"A farm," I repeated, trying to process the news.

"Yes!" She clapped her hands and had a little jig on the spot. "I'm starting my own business!"

However hard I tried, the image of Tawna as a farmhand wouldn't come. I could just about imagine her as a milkmaid, perched on a stool wearing a white dress with puffed-up sleeves, but even that was a push. I certainly didn't envisage her mucking out stables or rounding up sheep.

"Okay." The word stretched out like elastic as I played for time. "That sounds... exciting?"

Being enthusiastic was difficult when it sounded like a madcap idea. Tawna and a farm? It didn't make sense. However, the three of us had a pact to support each other and Eve looked over-the-moon happy for our friend, so I tried to follow her lead by forcing a smile of encouragement.

"So exciting. It's not the right time of year for tourists, of course," she babbled, "but that means we have plenty of time to get everything ready. And I've got so many ideas. Not that I'm going to go overboard."

"Because reining yourself in has always been your strength," Eve teased, earning herself a disapproving look from Tawna.

"You won't get a rise out of me, not this time. I'm going to put my heart and soul into this project, just you wait and see."

I had no doubt she would because Eve was right, it was all or nothing with Tawna. It had been the whole time I'd known her and there was no sign of that changing. And I had to admit she seemed very motivated about the whole farm thing for someone who had never been that into animals.

"We've been to get expert advice, with this being a new venture," she continued. "There's a lady down south who's done something similar and it's been a real success. Me and Johnny are going down next week to see her space, give us some ideas of how much it'll be realistic to do in the first year. Don't want to bite off more than we can chew."

"And you're sure about this? It's what you want?"

The unsaid words hung in the air. Tawna and Johnny had been trying for a baby so taking on a mammoth task like running a farm, especially when they had no clue about what it involved, seemed like a crazy decision. How would they cope if Tawna got pregnant? Johnny's business was already more than a full-time job.

"Of course it's what I want. You were the one who told me to make a go of the whole flower thing, well now I am."

Her chin jutted out, defiant.

"Flower thing..." I muttered, thinking out loud.

"Yes, a flower farm," she replied with a sigh, implying I was a fool for not understanding rather than her only telling half a story. "Johnny's bought half of a dairy farm that's been in a family for generations. The current owners are still going to live in the original farmhouse and run the dairy but Johnny's bought five acres. There's a crumbling old barn that he's going to do up so it can be an office and a shop. You're going to love it, Soph."

Her shoulders raised up to her ears as she gave a cheesy grin of excitement. "We're going to have fields of tulips and dahlias people can visit and I'm going to sell bouquets and bulbs and tubers. I can run workshops on flower arranging and making seasonal door wreaths too once I'm more confident. Then eventually we'd like to run a flower festival in one of the smaller fields."

I'd never seen her so driven. "That's amazing. You've thought of everything."

"I dream big," she said with a smile.

"There must be something in the air. It's not long since you got your new job, Eve, and Andrea's made a move back into art." I told them about her commission from the community centre and how now, in her sixties, she was taking her art seriously after so long on the back-burner. "Now Tawna's got a whole new business too. It's almost enough to make me feel like an underachiever."

"I'm not having that." Tawna waggled her finger. "It was you who gave me the idea to start with. Your determination to make a success of your crafting was a real inspiration to me."

I threw her a questioning look. "Hardly. I've not made anything for months. Everything's so busy and when I do get a moment to myself I'm too tired to even think about getting out my craft box."

"You *have* just had a baby," Eve reminded me, as though I might have forgotten. "Credit where credit's due."

"Last year I was booking craft fayres and Christmas markets." I'd been petrified at the time, worried people would think the things I made weren't good enough to sell. My concerns had been unfounded and I'd been pleasantly surprised with how well things had gone. "I haven't had time to make any new stock so no chance of that happening this year."

"I bet there are things you could make to sell that wouldn't take too long. Christmas decorations are always a winner," Eve suggested.

"Or cards," encouraged Tawna. "In fact, I was hoping you'd design business cards for the flower farm. We're going for a rustic look so don't want to go to a standard printers. We'll obviously pay you for it."

"Thank you for having faith in me, but I'm not sure. I've never done anything like that before."

But in spite of my doubts, my creative juices were already flowing. Ink stampers might work, a flower stamper on the left-hand side of the card and Tawna's details alongside. Christmas cards would be an option too; if I could come up with one or two simple designs and make them into packs it could be a winning idea. Not the variety of handmade goods I'd sold previously, but enough to keep my side hustle going and give me a much-needed boost.

"We'll talk about it another time," Tawna promised. "Once I've sorted out the branding for the business."

"Have you even got a name for it yet?" asked Eve.

Tawna nodded. "Flora by Tawna," she said proudly, before admitting, "It was going to be Flora and Fauna with Tawna until Johnny told me fauna isn't anything to do with flowers, it's animals or something." She shrugged dismissively. "And don't think I've forgotten that you got married without us, Soph. You've got a lot of making up to do."

She pouted dramatically.

"I tell you what, I know exactly how I can make it up to you." I smiled sweetly, hoping I was coming across as the picture of innocence. "How do you fancy taking charge of the flowers for the reception?"

OCTOBER

a football game? "It's a lovely idea, Dad." The line crackled as I pondered. "But I'm just not sure I'm ready for it yet."

"I know it's hard, pet, but sometimes the thought of doing something is worse than actually doing it. Scarlett will be absolutely fine for a few hours while you enjoy the match with your old dad."

She would be fine, I knew. It wasn't her I was worried about, it was me. Crowds of people intimidated me these days, and even though I knew the names of the people who'd sat around Dad's season ticket seat for years I couldn't relax. Which was madness really because even the people I didn't know by name I recognised by sight. They were almost an extension of my family, like distant cousins or something. Closer than that, really, seeing as I hadn't seen my cousins since my thirtieth birthday party.

"Don't think too hard about it, just say you'll come. In fact, tell you what, I won't even give you a choice. Kick off's at three and I'm meeting the usual crowd at the pub at one. I'll get to yours at half twelve, all right? And don't forget the lucky scarf," he added.

I didn't even have chance to reply before he hung up on me.

A sigh of despair came right from my toes at the thought of leaving Scarlett.

Back in the day there was nowhere I'd rather be on a Saturday at 3pm than at my beloved St James's Park. Watching Newcastle United had been a part of my life for so long and, until my teenage years when drunken adventures took over, it was my one big release. It was a community, a time to bond with my dad especially as neither of my siblings had ever got into football, despite Dad's best efforts.

Me, I'd loved it. It helped that I grew up during a golden age for the Toon. Shearer, Ginola, Beardsley. Playing in Europe was the norm, or so I thought. If the child back then knew the pinnacle was happening right in front of her eyes I'm not sure she would have believed it. But that's the thing about Newcastle United fans. Loyalty like nothing else. And however much we moan about how the game has become sanitised and monetised and driven by business rather than passion, we will always be completely committed to our team.

That was why I knew that, despite my doubts, I'd be joining my friends on the Gallowgate End.

"You don't mind me going, do you? My dad didn't really give me a chance to say no." It was the tenth time in as many minutes that I'd asked Max the same question.

"Go. Enjoy yourself. We'll be fine and you'll be back in time to watch *Strictly*."

"I don't want you to think I'm running out on you and Scarlett…"

"Go!" He was practically shooing me out of the door as Dad beeped the horn. "Don't even think about us. Have fun with your dad and your friends and we will see you at teatime. Hopefully in a good mood with three points in your back pocket."

"That'd be nice," I said with a smile, although Newcastle's form left a lot to be desired after a dreadful start to the season.

The excitement on Dad's face was enough to remind me why I wanted to come. Even though it was a warm day he was wearing a scarf and because he insisted he was too old to wear a football shirt, ridiculing the people of his age who wore the traditional black and white stripes, he had a black polo shirt with a club crest discreetly placed over his heart.

Being in the pub before the match wasn't the perfect fix, the chanting and general noise like something from a previous life after so long avoiding crowds.

My nerves jangled as I worried about what was happening at home, and even though I knew there was nothing to worry about I couldn't squash the feeling I'd thrown Max in at the deep end. Which was a ridiculous concept really, considering he was Scarlett's father and more than capable of looking after her.

Finley, wearing the latest shirt, bought me a bottle of Newky Brown. It was the first year in a long time I didn't have the newest kit. After having Scarlett it galled me to spend that amount of money on a shirt which was not that different to the one the team had worn the previous season and the one before that and the one before that. There's only so much a designer can do with black and white stripes. I hadn't expected my old shirt to fit after all my body had been through, but surprisingly it didn't look bad. Vertical stripes were supposed to be slimming, weren't they? Maybe they were working their magic.

If I hadn't known better I would have thought Dad had read my mind because the next thing he said to me was that we needed to go to the club shop so he could buy me the latest shirt.

I shook my head and protested. "You don't need to do that, Dad. Save your money for something else."

"Drew family tradition." The look he gave me was as if I'd forgotten the most basic of rules. "I always get you a new kit when it comes out."

"Honestly, it's fine. If you really want to get one maybe we should buy her first shirt." I didn't need to mention Scarlett's name; I knew Dad would know who I meant. "She's got the Babygro and a bib with a cartoon magpie saying 'me and my mummy support Newcastle United' but no actual shirt."

I'd seen my dad lots of times since having Scarlett but being back at St James's Park, a place that was so special to us both, was exactly what I needed. All those years where I dreamed of being an adult seemed a distant memory. Spending time with my dad was grounding. I didn't have to be a grown-up with him, I think he'd have been almost disappointed if I had been.

Our roles were very clear. Dad and daughter, with him the protector and me knowing I could rely one hundred per cent on him to keep me safe. Ever his little girl, always his Princess Sophie. And, rightly or wrongly, that was what I needed. Knowing that, just for those ninety minutes, there was no one relying on me to look after them.

The roar of the crowd as Joelinton scored was ear splittingly loud. The surge of adrenaline and the collective delight meant our group were hugging each other fiercely. Finley and Joel, me and Norma and Dad and Burley Bez.

"Can't see us throwing this away," Joel shouted above the cheers. "Think we might have a win in the bag here."

It wasn't a game for the ages, and passed with little drama and no further goalmouth action but that didn't matter a jot. As the referee blew his whistle and three sharp shrift peeps rang out around the stadium, the supporters were on their feet to applaud the team.

It didn't affect our position in the league, but three points and a winning feeling were always welcome.

"Are we going to The Strawberry for a quick one?" Norma asked as we joined the haphazard queue of people trying to exit the stands. "My shout."

"I should get back. Max has had Scarlett all day. If anyone deserves a drink it's him."

Just because I'd had a day away from the routine and the stresses of parenthood I hadn't forgotten what each long and tiring day felt like.

Over the months since Scarlett's birth I'd learned that it was normal to want to thrust your child at your partner the moment they walked through the door. It didn't mean I loved my daughter any less, all it meant was I needed a break. And that didn't need to be anything flash or fancy. Sometimes all I wanted was the opportunity to go to the toilet without balancing a baby on my lap.

"Call him," Dad suggested. "I bet he won't mind if you stay out a bit longer. We won't be more than an hour and I'll drop you back."

"Come on, Soph," Finley cajoled, pulling his lips into an over-exaggerated pout. "We hardly see you these days. A drink after the match for old time's sake?"

"Go on then," I agreed, tightening my lucky scarf around my neck. "So long as I get home in time for *Strictly*!"

CHAPTER 34

*A*s we prepared for our party I was grateful we hadn't had the ceremony on the same day. Setting up tables, draping bunting and fairy lights, listening to Tawna fuss about whether or not the flowers were up to standard and how she couldn't work fast enough was exhausting. When I tried to imagine how it would have been if I'd also been rushing to get ready for the ceremony, panicking about all eyes being on me, I knew we'd made the right decision.

"And you're sure the table arrangements aren't too small?" Tawna shuffled the three café au lait dinner plate dahlias that made up the centrepiece around the tall slim vase, which made no difference at all to how they looked (gorgeous – easy feathered petal a creamy-peach work of art). "I could always add more if you wanted a bigger statement. There are two more buckets full in the back of the car."

"They're perfect," I assured her. "Any more would be overkill."

"I don't want you to be disappointed with the flowers when you look back at the photos. You could have had a professional."

"But one of my best friends is training to be a florist and I'd rather think 'Tawna spent so long making sure the venue looked beautiful' when I look at the photos than them looking like every other wedding in the county."

She blew me a kiss across the table.

I reached my hand up to grab it and clutched it to my chest.

She glanced around the room, taking in the decorations. "Anything else need doing? Speak now, or forever hold your peace."

The pearlescent balloons were inflated (again in threes – Tawna insisted this was a must in terms of aesthetics, while I liked that it mirrored the number of people in our family unit), bunting shaped like autumn leaves strung from the oak beams. Sashes were wrapped around each chair, symmetrical bows hanging from their backs. Jars of penny chews, mint imperials and jelly sweets were lined up on a table along with pink and white candy-striped bags for guests to help themselves to treats when in need of a sugar rush.

Everything was just as I'd imagined it would be. All that was left to do was for me and Max to gather our loved ones and party well into the night.

"I think we're done."

Tawna held her hand up to me, my own palm connecting with hers in a victory high-five.

"Time to get pampered," she said, taking one final glance around the room. "Let's go!"

It felt good to wear my wedding dress again, both in terms of my own confidence and getting value for money. It hadn't been an extravagance in the way many brides dresses were, but I couldn't get out of the mindset that I needed to get a few wears in. I'd already decided that after the party I'd see if I could dye the dress to wear for Scarlett's naming day.

The deep pockets I'd so admired when first trying on the dress were going to come into their own as I'd made the decision to forget about a handbag, instead keeping a lipstick on my person. With Scarlett's changing bag a necessary accessory (although I didn't plan to be carting it around all evening, instead finding an out-of-sight corner where it would be easy to grab if needed but well out of the way when my husband decided to do the Macarena or whatever other organised dance he was in the mood for) I was keen to limit myself to the bare essentials.

Eve had styled my hair, copying the step-by-step guide of a YouTube video. She'd done a brilliant job and that along with the subtle contouring and make-up Tawna had helped me apply gave the illusion of the cheekbones I'd always coveted but never been blessed with.

I felt a million dollars as the three of us made our way down to the front room to travel to the venue with Max and Scarlett.

Each step was a sashay and as I walked along our hallway to the living room, the times I'd stood in the same spot, dreading walking into my own lounge, were a distant memory. Still there, still clear in my mind, but far enough removed it no longer caused pain.

I struck a pose as I reached the door frame, hand on my hip, head tilted to one side. Naomi, Kate and Co weren't going to be quaking in their crazily high heels but I didn't care about that. The look of admiration on my husband's face was all I needed.

"She looks stunning, doesn't she, girls?"

Eve and Tawna both replied in the affirmative, Scarlett joining in with the "mamamamamamama" noise she liked so much.

"That's right, your mama looks like a princess," Eve cooed, taking her from Max's arms. "Just like you."

Max had got Scarlett ready, the pretty dress she'd worn in Scotland getting another outing. She seemed to have more hair since the weeks had passed, and she'd been born with a shock of hair to start with. The baby headband, one Max had teased me mercilessly for buying from his charity shop, was coming in handy.

"Right," Max said, readjusting his collar when he caught sight of his reflection in the hall mirror, "are we ready?"

"That depends. Did you remember to put a change of clothes in Scarlett's bag? And some nappy sacks – I used the last one at baby massage yesterday."

"I thought you'd done the restock." He looked at me like I'd gone mad. "You told me the change bag was in the hallway."

I clucked my tongue against the roof of my mouth. "It is in the hallway. I didn't say it was ready though. That's why I was telling you where it was, so you could make sure it was ready."

"I'm not a mind reader."

An awkward glance passed between Eve and Tawna, caught in the middle of our domestic. "Shall we go out to the car?" Eve asked tentatively. "Leave you two to get the last few bits and pieces?"

"We're fine," I insisted, making my way to the utility room to grab a spare outfit for Scarlett. "This is just what it's like trying to get out of the house when you've got a five-month-old."

"Don't bicker, guys." Tawna threaded one arm through mine and her other through Max's as though she was the central link in a chain. "It's your wedding day. Or sort of wedding day. You know what I mean. It's a celebration, not a day for getting worked up over something as boring as what's in a changing bag."

I knew she was right, and I also knew that marriage was

going to be a lifetime of moments like this. Times when Max would leave the toilet seat up or a towel on the bathroom floor. Use the last of the milk and not think to replace it, or some other niggly issue that, whilst not a crime, would have me counting to ten in my head and muttering obscenities under my breath. And I wasn't a fool, it would be a two-way street. My hair would block the plughole in the shower, or I'd not clean the hob after cooking a fry-up and he'd grumble as he wiped the grease from the stainless-steel surface. It wouldn't mean we were any less in love. It would just mean we were human.

"You're right. We need to get moving if we're going to make it to the venue before the guests. I know it's traditional for a bride to be late for her wedding but I'm not sure it counts when it's the reception."

"It's your party so you two make the rules," Tawna insisted. "Just make sure you take time to soak it up. It'll fly by and you'll realise you've been so busy talking to all the guests that you haven't spent a minute together all night. Especially as you're not even doing the whole first dance thing."

"We'll see about that," I teased. "How do you know we've not been working on an elaborate showstopper routine with Anton du Beke?"

Max laughed. "Imagine! I don't think you'd trust me with some of those fancy lifts."

"We could give it a go…"

"*Dirty Dancing!*" Eve visibly swooned. The film had long been a favourite of us three girls. "Max can be Johnny Castle and you can be Baby."

I pursed my lips together, slowly shaking my head. "Sadly that won't be possible," I said with mock seriousness. "We did plan to practice in water, but Leazes Park lake looked cold so we gave it a miss."

"Very funny," Eve replied drolly, lifting Scarlett high above her head in a tribute to the very lift Patrick and Jennifer had made their own.

As we left the house, Max double checking the door was locked behind us, he whispered in my ear.

"Their minds will be well and truly blown when we get up on that dance floor."

And I knew he was right.

eing surrounded by the people we love was exactly what we'd hoped for. There were the family members we saw regularly, our closest friends who were as good as relatives, and those who we thought of often but didn't get chance to see because of distance or schedules. Finlay and Joel, friends from the days when I was a regular watching Newcastle United at St James's Park, were so happy for us, and some of the friends Max didn't spend as much time with as he'd like since becoming a dad.

There was a lovely vibe in the room with everyone wanting to offer their congratulations. My face ached from the non-stop smiling, and it wasn't long before the gentle fuzz of tipsiness took over – two glasses of Prosecco was all it took to give me a buzz these days.

Trestle tables covered in rustic hessian were laden with simple finger foods, triangular sandwich bites, slivers of pizza, bowls of olives and tortilla chips with salsa and guacamole dip; the pie and pea supper I'd promised Dad coming later in the evening to soak up the alcohol which would inevitably be supped.

The wedding cake was on a table of its own, a traditional three-tiered affair reminiscent of the one Tawna had arranged for my thirtieth birthday party (minus the pink icing – instead flowers topped each layer, the autumnal shades in stark contrast to the unblemished white icing). It was, quite rightly, gaining attention from the guests – they were probably desperate for us to get to the point where me and Max cut it so they could try a slice for themselves.

I knew they were in for a treat, having tried the samples. It had been difficult to choose a flavour as they'd all been mouth-wateringly delicious, from the chocolate fudge cake to the Seville orange sponge. In the end we'd opted for a traditional fruitcake which we were serving with double cream to enhance the raisin and sultana flavour.

Max's best friends were excellent musicians, well-known on the local circuit. Kindly they had offered to play two hour-long sets throughout the evening without charge, saying instead it was part of their wedding present to us. I'd seen them play live before and had no doubts that they'd have our guests up and dancing.

The rest of the night's music was a guest-led playlist, where we'd asked everyone to choose a song they loved. We'd had an eclectic mix put forward, everything from Aerosmith to Atomic Kitten, Meat Loaf to Madonna, Black Sabbath to Black Lace (I had my suspicions my husband would be busting some moves to the latter going on if Hector and Andrea's revelations were anything to go by).

"Congratulations!"

"You look beautiful, Sophie."

"I can't believe you eloped. That's so romantic."

Everyone was so kind, which made me, Max and Scarlett feel so supported. We were lucky to have so many amazing people in our lives, people who'd taken time out of their precious weekend to come and party with us.

My boss, Marcie, and her husband were the first on the dance floor, one of those couples who could jive a bit (and also, if I was being honest, they probably weren't out on the town every Saturday night). They hopped from foot to foot, waggling their hands at the bottom of their spines to make tail feathers, spinning each other around and gathering quite an audience.

More people arrived, a large pile of cards and gifts building up on the table near the entrance. We'd made it clear that we hadn't invited people for gifts (even using that little poem everyone puts on invites, the "your presence means more to us than your presents" one), but it appeared no one had listened.

Norma, bless her soul, had handed me a card with a warning to keep it on me as it had money inside. She looked older and frailer since Fred had passed away, but she still had all her marbles and her sense of fun had gone nowhere either. Joel and Finlay made sure she had a steady stream of her favourite port and lemon tipple (I wasn't even sure if the limited bar would stock something so dated, but Norma was in luck).

Kath, my work colleague, had brought a plus one, a distinguished, moustachioed man who had more than a hint of a look of a "Three Men and a Baby" era Tom Selleck. I'd done a double take at first, what with her usual post-divorce type being men who looked, and often were, much younger than her. Her ex had taken the route of setting up home with a twenty-nine-year-old and I'd always secretly wondered if Kath's sexual antics with men young enough to be her son were a form of revenge, even though he more than likely knew nothing about any of her conquests.

"It's nice to meet you," I said, shaking the hand of this stranger who I discovered was called Mickey. "We weren't expecting Kath to bring a plus-one."

"Until last night I'd not expected to be coming either," he said with a laugh, which made me think he was one of Kath's many one-night stands, which was a pity, because he came across as a real gentleman, attentive and caring, with his hand placed comfortingly, but not possessively, around her waist.

"So it's a new thing then? I thought it must be as Kath hadn't mentioned going on any dates." Jane, another of the women in my department at work, acted as though she despaired of Kath's flings, but in truth I think she loved the salacious gossip, so long as the details weren't too gory. We'd been exposed to all sorts of her escapades, from the backpacker with a Prince Albert piercing ("If you ever get the chance to sleep with a man who's had his cock pierced, go for it," she'd enthused. "I never believed in the G-spot before, but the friction from the metal bar gave me the best orgasm of my life.") to the student who'd eaten a chicken and mushroom pot noodle off her naked stomach ("As if the smell of his student digs wasn't bad enough," she'd complained the next day, chalking it down to experience).

"Actually, no. We've been seeing each other on and off for a long time."

"Forty years," Kath added, giving a fond look in Mickey's direction. "He was my first boyfriend at school. He stole my lunchbox."

I wasn't sure if that was a euphemism.

"I'd never kissed a girl before I kissed Kath," Mickey reminisced, gazing dreamily into Kath's eyes. "And although there were plenty more in between, none compared to her."

"We met up again when we were twenty," Kath continued, "but we were both married by then. We had a spark still, even though we were both with other people."

"Kath was the reason my first wife left me. Yvonne said I'd never got over my first love." Mickey pulled a face that suggested she was probably right. "I've been married twice more, but there was always a 'what if' when it came to me and Kath. When I heard she was divorced I asked a mutual friend to help us get back in touch."

"And now we're a couple." Kath beamed.

Jane blinked whereas Marcie actually gasped. Me, I was dumbstruck.

"Don't look so surprised," Kath said, pretending to be insulted. "I know you lot think of me as an old floozy but I'm the same as everyone else. I'm looking for my own happy ending."

The couple shared a look of love and it was impossible for me not to wonder if the talk of happy endings had sexual connotations too. Urgh.

"I'd better mingle. Bride duties." I waved my arm in a way that I hoped suggested I was in demand. "We're due to cut the cake soon. It's been lovely to meet you, Mickey."

"And you. Congratulations again on your marriage."

CHAPTER 36

My mind was still boggling when I ran into my brother, Nick, and his family at the sweet stall. My twin nieces, Imogen and Alicia, were too small for Black Jacks and Fruit Salads but Chantel had a sweet tooth and my nephew, Noah, took after his mum.

"Caught in the act," I said, placing my hands on my sister-in-law's shoulders.

She jumped back, guiltily dropping her stripy goodie bag, a mint imperial rolling towards the dance floor. Noah, not put off by the possibility of germs, chased the little white ball across the room.

"You made me jump," she panted, raising her hand to her chest. "My heart's racing."

"Sorry." I raised my hands up. "But you don't need to worry the sweets are there to be eaten. In fact, you'd be doing me a favour. I don't want to take them home, I'll only eat them and none of my clothes fit as it is."

"That's because you've just had a baby," she replied, sensibly. "A few sweets won't make a difference."

She held out the familiar pink and orange wrapper of a Fruit

Salad and I took it, unpeeling the waxy layer and placing the heavenly juicy rectangle in my mouth.

"You're probably right," I said, although with the chew already stuck between my teeth it sounded more like, "Yoush pwobly wight."

"You've done a great job with this, Bumface." My brother went to ruffle my hair but after all the effort that had gone into it I rapidly ducked out of the way. My bridesmaids would hit the roof if I had so much as a hair out of place after all their efforts.

"It wasn't me, this is Max's handiwork. There's a reason he's an award-winner, you know. Lots of experience of window dressing."

"And did I tell you you look fantastic? Almost as good as at that fancy dress party I had for my seventh birthday."

The wicked smile that went with his comment caused me to groan.

"Do we have to go over this again? It wasn't my fault. I was supposed to be going as a princess but I'd had a growth spurt and the bridesmaid's dress I'd worn for a family wedding didn't fit."

"We've all been there," Chanel said with a nonchalant shrug. "We had a Hallowe'en dress-up at work the other year that I'd forgotten all about until the night before. Ended up sticking on black leggings and T-shirt, a hairband with two triangles stuck to the top and drew whiskers on my face with eyeliner. I'd hoped to look like Bombalurina from 'Cats' but ended up more like a mangy old stray that'd been bin-digging for scraps."

"Sophie can go one better than that." My brother smirked. "Go on, tell Chantel what you'd come as."

My hands met my forehead, the realisation I wasn't going to get away without sharing the story hitting hard.

"I panicked. The party was at our house and mum was so

busy putting all the layers of wrapping on the pass the parcel that she told me it didn't matter if I didn't have fancy dress."

"But Sophie didn't want to be the odd one out," Nick chipped in gleefully. "So she decided to find her own fancy dress."

"All right, all right, I was getting to the punchline."

"There was nothing suitable in my own wardrobe. I had school uniform, but I wasn't a big fan of Britney's 'One More Time' video, and why would I want to wear a school uniform on a weekend? I had to wear it all week. Nick and Anna's clothes were never going to fit so I went into Mum and Dad's room to see what I could find. There were all the usual boring things, so I ignored those, but in the chest of drawers by the bed there were more interesting things."

Nick chortled, knowing what was coming.

Chantel raised her eyebrows, "Go on..."

"There was a nurse's outfit there. I thought it was strange at the time, because Mum wasn't a nurse, and it wasn't hung up in the wardrobe with the rest of her clothes. I thought it'd be far too big for me because obviously she was my mum and adult-sized and I was only young. But even though it was long, it wasn't dragging along the floor or anything. There was even an old-fashioned nurse's hat and stethoscope. I'd never seen a nurse wearing one of those hats in real life, but I put it on anyway and waited by the door to let everyone in. Mum was still busy in the kitchen. I thought I was being really helpful."

"It would have been all right if the stitching on the breast pocket didn't say 'Nurse Love – Makes more than your heart throb'." Nick laughed. "One of my friend's mums said she needed a word with Mum and I remember Sophie being sent upstairs to get changed."

"I cried my eyes out," I admitted. "I was enjoying wearing my fancy dress. It was only as I got older that I realised it was from Mum and Dad's 'special drawer'." I drew air quotes with my fingers as I grimaced. Thinking about your parents getting down to business was embarrassing enough, but imagining them role playing in the bedroom was even worse. "She told me to put on my pyjamas and come as Wee Willie Winkie, which didn't impress me much. I was far too old for nursery rhymes and was at the age where 'wee', 'willie' and 'winkie' were all rude words."

"The best thing about it was Mum was so busy apologising to Jordan's mum that she'd left us unsupervised with the food. We'd demolished the lot by the time she got back. Cake included."

Chantel laughed. "That's a life lesson right there. Lockable drawers for anything you don't want the children finding." Then, as though realising I, her sister-in-law, was there, added, "Not that we have anything like that."

If ever there was a good time to make my excuses, that was it, but Max was waving over at me, knife in hand to signal it was time to cut the cake. It was either that or he was recreating a *Hammer House of Horrors* classic.

Everyone gathered round to watch the cutting of the cake, a moment I'd always found marginally disappointing at the weddings I'd been to because it usually meant pushing onto tiptoes to even try to see what was going on or, if trying to document the moment for posterity, holding my phone above my head and hoping for the best as I pressed the button to capture the image.

Ours was better though. For a start, I could see the cake close up. The scent of sugar mixed with a hint of fresh floral aroma, it reminded me of happiness.

Tawna's words of wisdom about making sure Max and I spent time together came to mind as we pressed the blade through the fruitcake. I was determined to make as many memories as possible.

Glancing around at our loved ones watching on with pride

sent a warm glow running through me. My mum and dad, arms around each other with huge smiles on their faces. Andrea snapping away on her camera phone as Hector – chair spruced up with Christmas lights, just as he'd promised – held Scarlett, who was already changed out of her first outfit, I noticed. All five of our siblings and their families, clapping and cheering, with many others from all parts of our life joining in.

My eyes connected with Eve's as she held tightly to her mum's hand. How much Lucille, who had been as much of a mum to me as my own mum had during the awkward teenage years, would remember about the day was questionable. Her short-term memory was lapsing, although she talked fondly of the past. Often she'd mention her work, as though she still had a job to go to, and thought she and Eve's dad, Greg, were still a couple.

To be fair, although they'd barely been in touch over the years other than to talk about Eve, Greg had stepped up to support his daughter as she looked after her mum. It was difficult with him living and working in London, but he'd made regular visits to see Lucille in the care home, playing her the reggae tracks they'd listened to on repeat during their romance from a Spotify playlist he'd made especially.

There was something about that, the modern version of a traditional mixtape, that caused my heart to clench. Music is the closest thing we have to a time machine, songs so intrinsically linked to a time or place. It was the greatest gift he could have given her, far more useful than a box of biscuits or a bunch of flowers.

Tawna and Johnny were raising their glasses in a toast, talking to Nadia and Summer, who looked very pretty in her bridesmaid dress. She was on the cusp – still young and cute, and her vaguely precocious nature was charming rather than annoying. It wouldn't be long though before puberty struck her, hormones and acne and period pains changing her into a woman rather than a girl.

Life changes in the blink of an eye, I realised. No amount of planning helps, because there are surprises – some pleasant, some less so – around each and every corner. Illness, pregnancy, finances, plain old ageing. They all take their toll and we have to choose whether to let them floor us or roll with the punches, which inevitably means taking a painful smack in the mouth once in a while.

Finally, I turned to Max. Our relationship had propelled forward at breakneck speed after discovering I was expecting Scarlett, but I was confident we would have reached this point regardless, just perhaps slightly further down the line.

He accepted me, flaws and all.

More than that, he loved me, flaws and all.

And as we jointly held up the first slice of wedding cake, posing for a cheesy photo of us both taking a bite from it, I knew that whatever surprises life threw at us, we'd tackle them together.

The opening bars of DJ Casper's one-hit wonder "Cha Cha Slide" played out from the speakers.

"Are you dancing, Mrs Oakley-Drew?" Max held out his hand.

"Are you asking, Mr Oakley-Drew?" I quipped, reaching out for my husband's hand.

And that was our first dance. The first of many.

FEBRUARY

EPILOGUE

The first litter we visited were super-cute – fur of marbled merle and sparkling eyes as round as pennies. Four balls of fluff wobbling on their little legs like drunkards, jumping at each other with a lack of finesse. They were everything puppies should be, playful and energetic and full of fun.

"Look at this little one." I glanced underneath to see if it was a male or a female. "Hello, sweet boy," I said, as his muzzle nuzzled against my neck. His coat was cotton-wool soft.

"He is gorgeous," Max admitted, coming closer to fuss the pup.

I didn't normally stoop so low, but using my feminine wiles was a tactic I thought might just pay off. Eyelashes were fluttered. I talked in my babyish voice. Anything to get Max to cave.

Even though the puppy was officially my birthday present, he wanted a dog as much as I did, so I didn't expect to need to push too hard. Puppies as sweet as these were difficult to resist, and as the breeder went to fetch the paperwork to show the puppy I'd fallen for had been to the vets for his first injections I pleaded with Max.

"I'm in love." The warmth of the fur against my cheek was better than any comfort blanket. "Can we?"

The man returned before Max could answer, armed with paperwork and reminding us of the price and how we'd be able to take the pup home in a fortnight's time.

We baulked at the price, but they were all so adorable and the one had already stolen my heart. Even though I was cautious with money I would have paid up on the spot if it hadn't been for Max telling the breeder we'd go away and think about it.

I'd spent the journey home pouting and huffing, until he'd explained his doubts.

"The mother wasn't there. We can't buy a dog without seeing the mum. Puppy farms are rife."

"That wasn't a puppy farm." I laughed. "It was a normal house belonging to a normal family. There were photos of the kids on the wall and everything."

"You can't be too careful. That's what they do. Make you think you're buying from nice people when the puppies are aggressively bred and kept in awful conditions. Worse still, they aren't health tested. Some of these dogs end up with all kinds of nasty diseases and deformities."

"They weren't deformed! They were perfect!" I already felt a need to protect the little fur babies.

"They were all very cute and I can see why you want one, but if we're going to spend that amount of money on a dog we need to make sure they're not going to end up a) in pain and b) costing us a fortune in vet's bills. We'll keep looking – the right dog for us will be out there somewhere."

"That was the right dog for us," I grumbled, my grumpiness coming to the fore. I'd been getting ahead of myself, imagining

Scarlett and the pup to be best friends as they grew up. "I even had a name ready. Poochie. He looked like a Poochie."

"There's no way any dog of ours is being called that. We'll be calling their name across a park for years to come."

My arms automatically folded across my chest. I was acting like a brat just because I couldn't get my own way. "Fine." I turned my head away from him, looking purposefully out of the window as we passed a run of shops. A bakery, one of the chain ones. A bookies. A card shop and a Post Office. Nothing out of the ordinary but I acted as though they were captivating.

Max flicked on the radio. The song that blasted out was unfortunate, both because of its theme and its annoyingly catchy chorus. Baha Men's classic "Who Let the Dogs Out".

Against my grumpiness I couldn't help but laugh. The timing couldn't have been better (or worse, depending on how you looked at it).

"When we get back we'll start searching again. Promise." Max took his eyes off the road for a moment and smiled reassuring at me.

But I still thought of little Poochie and hoped he'd find a home where his family would love him as much as I would have.

"There's a litter of French Bulldog/pug crosses in Sunderland?"

"No, no and nope. Those squashed faces cause all kinds of breathing problems, that's why they wheeze."

"Golden labs near York?" Auntie Trish had a Labrador when I was growing up and he was a really good-natured dog, it was what had led her to get a Labradoodle in Australia.

"Something smaller would be better. Surely there are more cockapoos? They're all I see out and about."

"There are miniature poodles here, born four weeks ago. Are

they the smallest ones? I'm never sure if it's miniatures or toys that are the really little ones."

I scrolled through the photos attached to the link. First up was a picture of a well-groomed white poodle laying on a fleecy orange blanket surrounded by a patchwork of puppies. The next was a close up of the same poodle, labelled "mum", with a third of a tightly curled red poodle marked as "dad". Then came the shots of the pups, a mixture of auburn, apricot and white cuties. They were adorable and I leant across to show Max the pictures. The final picture made me gasp, somehow I knew the puppy in the photo was meant to join our family. Creamy-white fur in tight whorls, two perfectly round black eyes peering out above a shiny black nose.

My heart clenched in my chest. I didn't want to show Max my desperation but at the same time I already loved the puppy. When people talk about a gut feeling, that was the reaction, physiological.

"They're sweet," Max agreed, although it would be impossible to think otherwise. The baby poodles looked like little spring lambs. "And only a couple of miles down the road. Give them a call and see if we can go and view them."

I was scared to make the call in case the little puppy was already reserved.

I needn't have worried. "You're the first call we've had. Two of the apricot pups are already reserved by people who were on a waiting list but the other five are available. They're a lovely litter and Mum's doing a wonderful job."

An hour later we were there, Scarlett mesmerised by the bounding balls of fur.

"All males except that little red one," the man told us, pointing to the runt. "She's taking her time catching up. Couldn't get the hang of feeding at all, ended up having to give her formula from a bottle. We had alarms going off in the middle of the night to get up and feed her and all sorts."

"No alarms needed here, but we know the feeling." I was able to laugh about my exhaustion, in a black humour kind of way. We were nowhere near Scarlett sleeping through the night but having a good four-hour run of uninterrupted sleep most nights made all the difference.

The puppy I'd fallen head over heels for made a beeline for us, his run like Bambi, ungainly and unstable. He looked up at us, his eyes full of expectation and my heart did that flip flop that happens so rarely, the unmistakable sign of falling in love.

Max held out the back of his hand and the puppy sniffed, his damp nose drawing a zigzagged line from Max's wrist to his knuckles.

My husband lifted the squirming puppy into his arms, the inquisitive twitchy nose taking in the scent of Max's jumper and neck and face.

I could tell by his laughter he was as taken as I was. Scarlett was fascinated too, her gaze following the puppy's every movement.

Ten minutes later, once Max had asked the questions he'd prepared and had satisfactory answers, we were paying a holding deposit and arranging to visit again the following week so the puppy could get to know us before we took him home to Anderson Green.

As we were saying our goodbyes, the breeder asked if we had a name in mind.

Max shook his head, but from nowhere I found myself making a suggestion.

"How about Blue?"

It suited him, and I liked that with Blue and Scarlett we would have our own colour scheme going on.

A smile of approval broke out on Max's face.

"Blue. I like it. He looks like a Blue."
Sophie, Max, Scarlett and Blue.
A winning team. Team Oakley-Drew.
And, just like that, our family was complete.

THE END

ACKNOWLEDGMENTS

When I set out to write about Sophie and her friends I planned a trilogy – and here we are at the end of book three! A lot has changed in Sophie's life throughout the books and, unsurprisingly, a lot has changed in mine too. Back in summer 2017 we had no idea of what was coming...

Writing during a pandemic didn't come easily to me and for that reason I'll be eternally grateful to the supportive bunch below who were cheerleaders throughout.

The team at Bloodhound Books, with special thanks to Betsy Reavley, Tara Lyons and Morgen Bailey for their support and hard work.

Poppy Alexander, Philippa Ashley, Mary Jayne Baker, Sarah Bennett, Rachel Burton, Brigid Coady, Miranda Dickinson, Rachel Dove, Lynsey James, Josie Silver, Keris Stainton, Inky Willis and all the Wordcount Warriors, A***-Kickers and Beta Buddies for always having my back.

The book blogger/vlogger/bookstagram community for being so enthusiastic about Sophie Drew.

My friends and family – especially Jenny King who jokingly suggested the spinoff 'A Cockapoo for Sophie Drew'.

Most of all, thank you to all of you, for choosing to spend time in Sophie's world. I hope you've enjoyed it.

Katey Lovell, Sheffield, November 2021

A NOTE FROM THE PUBLISHER

Thank you for reading this book. If you enjoyed it please do consider leaving a review on Amazon to help others find it too.

We hate typos. All of our books have been rigorously edited and proofread, but sometimes mistakes do slip through. If you have spotted a typo, please do let us know and we can get it amended within hours.

info@bloodhoundbooks.com

www.ingramcontent.com/pod-product-compliance
Lightning Source LLC
Chambersburg PA
CBHW020803190726
48285CB00006B/2145